Tracy Flick Can't Win

A Novel

Tom Perrotta

SCRIBNER

New York   London   Toronto   Sydney   New Delhi

Scribner
An Imprint of Simon & Schuster, Inc.
1230 Avenue of the Americas
New York, NY 10020

First Scribner hardcover edition June 2022

SCRIBNER and design are registered trademarks of The Gale Group, Inc.,
used under license by Simon & Schuster, Inc., the publisher of this work.

For information about special discounts for bulk purchases,
please contact Simon & Schuster Special Sales at 1-866-506-1949
or business@simonandschuster.com.

The Simon & Schuster Speakers Bureau can bring authors to your live event.
For more information or to book an event, contact the Simon & Schuster Speakers Bureau
at 1-866-248-3049 or visit our website at www.simonspeakers.com.

Manufactured in the United States of America

1   3   5   7   9   10   8   6   4   2

Library of Congress Cataloging-in-Publication Data

Names: Perrotta, Tom, 1961– author.
Title: Tracy Flick can't win : a novel / Tom Perrotta.
Other titles: Tracy Flick can not win
Description: First Scribner hardcover edition. | New York : Scribner, 2022.
Identifiers: LCCN 2021059411 | ISBN 9781501144066 (hardback) |
ISBN 9781501144080 (ebook)
Subjects: BISAC: FICTION / Humorous / General | FICTION / Family Life / General
Classification: LCC PS3566.E6948 T73 2022 | DDC 813/.54—dc23
LC record available at https://lccn.loc.gov/2021059411

ISBN 978-1-5011-4406-6
ISBN 978-1-5011-4408-0 (ebook)

Tracy Flick
Can't Win

The Hall of Fame is a tremendous, tremendous honor.
—Joe Montana

Now we got bad blood.
—Taylor Swift

PART ONE:

I Know That Guy

- 1 -

Tracy Flick

There was another front-page story in the paper. For months it had been an almost daily occurrence, one powerful man after another toppled from his pedestal, exposed as a sexual predator: Harvey Weinstein in his bathrobe, Bill Cosby with his quaaludes, Matt Lauer and his secret button; the list went on and on. It was a satisfying spectacle—a small measure of belated justice—but it was troubling too, because it kept stirring up memories I would have preferred to leave alone, as if I were being asked to explain myself to the world, though I wasn't exactly sure who was doing the asking.

That morning's scandal was celebrity-free, and for me, at least, even more disturbing than usual: a "beloved" drama teacher at a fancy boarding school accused of having "inappropriate sexual and romantic relationships" with several former students, the allegations stretching all the way back to the 1980s. The teacher—he was retired now, living quietly in Tulum—denied the charges; a lawsuit had been filed against the school, its trustees, and three different headmasters who had "abetted the decades-long cover-up." There was a black-and-white yearbook photo of the teacher in his younger days—he was standing onstage, boyish and shaggy-haired, directing a student production of *Oklahoma!*—along with color photos of two of his accusers. The women were attractive and successful, both around my own age—a dermatologist and an art historian—and they gazed at

3

the camera with eyes that were somehow steely and wounded at the same time. *He groomed me so skillfully,* the art historian said. *He told me exactly what I wanted to hear.* The dermatologist had a bleaker assessment: *He stole my innocence. It pretty much ruined my life.*

"Mom," Sophia said. "Are you okay?"

I looked up from the newspaper. My ten-year-old daughter was watching me closely from across the table, the way she often did, as if she were trying to figure out who I was and what was going on in my head. I'd never had to do that with my own mother.

"I'm fine, honey."

"It's just—you looked a little angry."

"I'm not angry. That's just how my face gets when I'm thinking." She considered this for a second or two, then wrinkled her nose.

"There's a name for that," she said. "It's not very nice, though."

"So I've heard." I glanced at the wall clock. "Finish your oatmeal, sweetie. We need to get moving."

Aside from the handful of people who knew about it at the time—my mother, the Principal, my guidance counselor—I never talked to anyone about what happened to me in high school. Until the past few months, I hardly even thought about it anymore, because what was the point? It was ancient history, a brief misguided affair—that's the wrong word, I know, but it's the one I've always used—with my sophomore English teacher, a few regrettable weeks of my teenage life. It wasn't that big a deal. We made out a few times, and had sex exactly once. I realized it was a mistake, and I ended it. My life wasn't ruined. I didn't get pregnant, didn't get my heart broken, didn't miss a step. I graduated at the top of my class, and went to Georgetown on a full scholarship.

It was Mr. Dexter who couldn't handle the breakup, and kept pestering me to get back together. My mother found a note he wrote on one of my essays—it was a little unhinged—and she went to the Principal, and Mr. Dexter vanished from the school, and from my life. It was all very sudden and surgical. I guess you could say the system worked.

As a grown-up—as a parent and an educator—I had no doubt that what he did was wrong, and that his punishment was just. In the privacy of my own heart, though, I couldn't manage to hate him for it, or even judge him that harshly. There was a mitigating factor at work, an extenuating circumstance. It didn't exonerate him, exactly, but it made him less culpable in my eyes, more worthy of sympathy or compassion, whatever you want to call it.

That circumstance was me.

The thing you had to understand—it seemed so obvious to me at the time, so central to my identity—is that I wasn't a normal high school girl. I was unusually smart and ambitious, way too mature for my own good, to the point where I had trouble making friends with my peers, or even connecting with them in a meaningful way. I felt like an adult long before I came of legal age, and it had always seemed to me that Mr. Dexter simply perceived this truth before anyone else, and had treated me accordingly, which was exactly the way I'd wanted to be treated. How could I blame him for that?

That was my narrative, the one I'd lived with for a very long time, but it was starting to feel a little shaky. You can't keep reading these stories, one after the other, all these high-achieving young women exploited by teachers and mentors and bosses, and keep clinging to the idea that your own case was unique. In fact, it had become pretty clear to me that that was how it worked—you got tricked into feeling more exceptional than you actually were, like the normal rules no longer applied.

It gnawed at me that summer, the possibility that I'd misjudged my own past, that maybe I'd been a little more ordinary than I would have liked to believe. But even if that were true, there wasn't anything I could do about it. There was no injustice to expose, no serial abuser living it up in a tropical paradise.

Mr. Dexter didn't just lose his job because of me; he lost his wife and a lot of his friends and his self-respect, and he never really got back on track. After he stopped teaching, he managed his family's hardware store until it went out of business, and then he became a home inspector. He got married a second time in his forties, but that hadn't worked out, either. I knew this because he wrote me a letter in 2014. He was in the hospital at the time, being treated for an aggressive form of prostate cancer, and wanted to apologize to me before it was too late. He said he still thought about me sometimes, and wished we'd met under different circumstances.

I'm not a bad person, he said. *I just made some horrible decisions.*

He was fifty-five when he died. As far as I was concerned, he could rest in peace.

Sophia was attending soccer camp that week at Green Meadow High School, where I served as Assistant Principal. I pulled up in the horse-shoe driveway by the practice field, idling just long enough to watch her sign in with a clipboard-wielding counselor, and then trot onto the grass, where she was greeted with a fanfare of happy shrieks and joyful shimmies from the other girls, as if they hadn't seen her for years. I felt a familiar pang of separation, the melancholy awareness that my daughter's real life—at least her favorite parts—took place in my absence.

I'd never been like that as a child, a valued member of the pack, showered with affection, protected by the safety of numbers. I'd always been a party of one, set apart from the other kids by the conviction—I possessed it from a very early age—that I was destined for something bigger than they were, a future that mattered. I didn't believe that anymore—how could I, my life being what it was—but I remembered the feeling, almost like I'd been anointed by some higher authority, and I missed it sometimes. It had been an adventure, growing up like that, knowing in my blood that something amazing was waiting for me in the distance, and that I just needed to keep moving forward in order to claim it.

The only thing waiting for me that morning was my cramped office in the empty high school, the unceasing demands of a job I'd outgrown. It was an important position, don't get me wrong—I had a lot on my shoulders—but it was hard to stomach being the number two again, after savoring an all-too-fleeting taste of real authority.

Three years earlier, I'd taken over as Acting Principal after my boss, Jack Weede, had suffered a near-fatal heart attack. He was sixty-five at the time, and everyone assumed he would pack it in, and that my promotion would become permanent. But Jack surprised us all by coming back; he couldn't let go of the reins. It was his call and I didn't hold it against him—retirement had never struck me as much of a prize, either—but the ordeal had taken a toll on him, and a lot of his workload ended up landing on good old Tracy's desk.

Even on a slow day in early August, there was more than enough to keep me busy. I started by combing through the analytics from our most recent round of assessment tests, trying to spot gaps in our curriculum, and offer some low-impact, last-minute suggestions for addressing them. We'd been slipping a bit in the statewide rankings—not badly, but just enough to cause some alarm—and we needed to take some concrete measures to turn that around before it became a serious problem.

After that, I scoured a stack of old résumés in search of a long-term substitute for Jeannie Kim, our popular (if slightly overrated) AP Physics teacher, who was taking maternity leave in January. An incompetent sub isn't a huge problem if they're only in contact with the students for a day or two, but Jeannie was going to be out for an entire semester.

If I'd left it up to Jack, he would've waited until the last minute, hired the first warm body he could get his hands on, and then shrugged it off if something went wrong. *It's hard to find a good sub, Tracy. There's a reason those people don't have real jobs.* But I wasn't about to let that happen, not if I could help it. Our students deserved better. It was easy to forget, when you were a grown-up and high school was safely in the past, how it felt to be a captive audience, the way time could stand still in a classroom, and one bad teacher could poison your entire life.

- 2 -

Vito Falcone was ready to make amends. With the help of his sponsor—a sullen Uber driver/piano teacher named Wesley—he'd drawn up a list of the people he'd wronged in a significant way. There were nineteen names on it, and that was just his adult life. He'd been a dick in middle school, and an even bigger dick in high school, but Wesley advised him to set that aside for the time being.

"You got your hands full as it is," he said.

It was a humbling experience for anyone—dredging up the past like that—but it was even worse for Vito, because . . . well, because he was *Vito*, an important person, well-known and widely respected, at least in some quarters. He'd played in the NFL for three seasons—not a superstar, but he'd shown a lot of promise until a knee injury ended his career—and he'd stuck with the game after his retirement, becoming one of the most successful high school coaches in central Florida. He was an alpha dog, the guy who gave the orders and let you know when you fucked up. The world was like this: you apologized to Vito; Vito didn't apologize to you. Nobody else in the church basement had any idea what that felt like, or how hard it was to surrender that kind of authority.

Of course, that was how you got into trouble in the first place—he understood that now—thinking you were more important than other people, or better than they were, and didn't have to follow the usual rules. But that was how Vito had lived his life, ever since the age of twelve, when he'd had his big growth spurt, and everyone suddenly realized what a freakishly gifted athlete he was. He'd been good-looking too—still was, for a guy in his midforties—and that

9

didn't help. Girls and women had always fallen into his lap; he didn't have to be nice to them, didn't even have to pretend. It wasn't healthy growing up like that, everybody acting like your shit didn't stink, because after a while you started to believe it too, and a person like that could do a lot of damage.

The other problem with believing you're special is the shock that comes when you finally realize you're not, that you're just as fucked up as everyone else, if not worse. For Vito, this reckoning had sunk in slowly over the past couple of years, when he'd begun to suspect that there was something wrong with his brain. He'd been having headaches for a while—bad ones—but then he started having these weird mental lapses. He'd be driving somewhere and he'd just zone out—he had no idea if it was a few seconds or a few minutes—and when he emerged from the fog, sometimes he wouldn't know where he was, or where he'd been going. He'd have to pull over and think about it, and the answer didn't always come to him right away. That was a terrible feeling, like his mind was an empty closet.

He knew about traumatic brain injuries, CTE, whatever you wanted to call it. Nobody involved with high school football could ignore that stuff, not anymore. And yeah, he'd had a concussion or three over the years. There was no way for a quarterback to avoid it. You'd set up in the pocket, start scanning downfield for receivers, and—*Bam!*—the lights would go out. Next thing you knew, you'd be standing on the grass with this woozy drone in your head while your teammates slapped you on the helmet, asking if you were okay, and you'd say yes, because that was the only possible answer. And if nobody stopped you, you went right back in the huddle and kept on playing, letting the autopilot take over until the cobwebs cleared—sometimes it took ten minutes, sometimes a couple of days—and then you'd forget all about it, because it did you no good to remember.

Vito didn't tell anyone about his lapses—not his doctor, not even his wife—because putting his fears into words would have made them real, and he didn't want them to be real. He wanted it to be like that time in college when he looked down and saw that he was pissing blood, a dark crimson river streaming out of him, like a Stephen King nightmare. He hadn't told anyone about that, and the next day he was back to normal.

I'm fine, he'd tell himself. *There's nothing wrong with me.*

But then it would happen again—Vito sweating on the side of the road, trying to remember where he was—and he knew he was fucked. And not in the normal way, like when he blew out his knee for the second time. That had sucked beyond belief—to be twenty-five years old and to know with absolute certainty that your dream was dead—but it wasn't the end of the world. Vito had gotten depressed for a while, and then he picked himself up and stepped into the next chapter of his story.

But *this*—this shit with his brain—was different. There was no next chapter with this. You were just a middle-aged guy in the old folks' home, a fifty-year-old drooling into a paper cup, waiting all day for visitors who aren't coming. It would be like you'd gone extinct, or maybe like you'd never existed at all.

Somehow he made it through football season, but things had gotten worse over the winter. He didn't feel like himself, and being stuck at home with his family didn't help. It was too quiet in the house, and the quiet would get him thinking, and then he'd start to spiral.

Drinking helped a little. A lot, actually, because if you were drunk and your brain malfunctioned, you could blame it on the alcohol. And if you were hung over, you couldn't worry too much about the future. It took all your energy and concentration just to make it through the day.

He spent a lot of time at the Instant Replay, a sports bar where he knew the owners. It felt good to be out of the house with a game on and people to talk to, all kinds of welcome distractions. But he was a public figure and needed to be careful about gossip, so some nights he hid out in the Last Call, a gloomy dive where he was often the young-est customer by twenty years. No one bothered him there, which was a relief when it wasn't depressing. Other times he just parked by the lake and listened to the radio, sipping Maker's from a flask.

It got bad in the spring. He made some careless mistakes at work—he was Athletic Director as well as Head Football Coach at St. Francis Prep—and got locked into an unpleasant dynamic with his wife, who alternated between accusing him of having an affair—not a terrible guess, considering his history—and begging him to see a therapist. And then, one night in May, it all came to a head at the dinner table.

"Vito," Susie snapped. "Did you hear a word your daughter just said?"

"Most of it," he lied. "I just missed the last bit."

Actually, Vito was a little buzzed and had been frantically trying to remember the name of a Will Ferrell movie, a really popular one he'd seen three or four times. He was pretty sure it started with an *S*, but it wasn't *Semi-Pro*, it was the other one, the one with the frat. He could've just looked it up on his phone, but he hated relying on Google to tell him something he already knew.

"It was about softball," said Henry, who was eight and small for his age.

Vito turned to his daughter. Jasmine was ten, already beautiful like her mom, and very emotional, also like her mom. He could see she was upset.

"I'm sorry, honey. What were you saying?"

"Nothing." She looked down at her plate. "Forget it."

"Come on," he said. "Don't be like that."

He reached across the table for her hand, but she yanked it away, and just like that it came to him: *Old School*. Jesus Fucking Christ. *Old School*. His body flooded with relief.

"The coach made her play second base," Henry explained.

"Hannah Park's the pitcher now." Susie lifted her eyebrows like this was supposed to mean something to Vito. "We thought maybe you could talk to the coach."

Vito was all caught up now, back on solid ground.

"No way. I'm not gonna talk to the coach. I can't interfere—"

"Vito," Susie said. "Just talk to the man. You don't have to—"

Vito shook his head. This was a matter of principle.

"I know it's hard," he told his daughter. "But you have to respect the coach's decisions. A team isn't a democracy. You understand that, right?"

"I'm better than Hannah," Jasmine whined.

Vito spoke calmly and matter-of-factly, the same way he did with his own players when they challenged his authority.

"Honey," he said. "Don't kid yourself. If you were better than Hannah, you'd still be starting pitcher."

To the best of Vito's recollection—and he'd had to recollect this moment a lot in the past few months—things got really quiet around the table, and then Jasmine burst into tears. Susie glared at him in disbelief.

"What the fuck, Vito?"

"What?" he said. "I'm just saying—"

She tapped her index finger against her forehead. "Is something wrong with your brain?"

"What? Whoa." Vito froze, his body flooding with adrenaline. "Don't even joke about that."

"I'm not joking," she told him.

It wasn't premeditated, he was sure of that. It was more like a reflex, like his hand had a mind of its own.

That wasn't me, he said, the first time he told his story at a meeting. *I love my wife. I'm not the kind of man who would do that.*

The second time he skipped the bullshit.

I slapped her pretty hard. Almost knocked her off the chair. And now I'm living in a shitty apartment by the highway, trying to clean up the mess I made.

That was a good first step, telling the truth about himself, acknowledging the pain he'd inflicted. And now it was time to apologize.

- 3 -

Jack Weede

It's hard to give up your life's work, especially if you've had some success. I know, Principal of a midsize suburban high school isn't the same as Senator or Judge or CEO, but it's something, and it becomes your identity. Let go of that and you become a smaller, sadder person. Just ask King Lear.

Nevertheless, the inevitable day of reckoning arrives. For me it came on a humid morning in late August, a week before the beginning of the new school year. My wife and I were standing in the parking lot of Green Meadow Medical Associates, both of us crying—not an uncommon occurrence after her appointments—except that on this particular morning we were crying with joy and relief. Alice had beaten the odds; her five-year cancer screen had come back clean.

"Let's do it," she said, clutching my wrists and smiling through her tears. "Let's hit the road."

Hit the road was our code for buying an RV and cruising around America, visiting the national parks and other points of interest. Not a very original fantasy, I know, but it had kept us going through the dark days of chemo, the wigs and support groups, the false positive that threw her into a tailspin that lasted for six months. On nights when Alice couldn't sleep—there had been so many—we'd lie awake and plot out the trip: *We'll do Glacier in the summer and Yosemite in*

15

the fall. We'll cook when we feel like it and eat out when we don't. We'll learn how to fly-fish and do the crossword every morning.

"I'm serious, Jack." The disease had aged her in a hundred cruel ways, but there was something girlish and hopeful in her expression that moved me deeply. "Now's the time."

Just to be clear, the motor home was more her dream than mine. I was happy to indulge her—it was the least I could do—but I never thought it would actually happen.

"Okay," I said. "Sure. Let's do it."

"Really?" She wiped her nose and gave me a skeptical look, which I knew I deserved. "You're actually gonna retire?"

"It's time," I said. "It's been time for a while now."

"You mean *right now*, or—?"

"No, no, in June," I clarified. "I can't just leave them in the lurch at the last minute. That wouldn't be fair to anyone. I'm the Principal."

"Tracy can take over. She's already done it once. You said yourself—"

"Honey," I said. "It's just one more year."

"Fine." She gave a grudging nod. "You'll retire in June. That's a deal, right?"

"Absolutely," I said. "Scout's honor."

We drove straight to the Winnebago dealership on Route 36. We knew the exact model we were looking for—it was part of the fantasy—and they had one in stock, a sleek Class A behemoth in dark maroon, a lumbering vacation home on wheels. After we signed the papers, I went home and wrote a letter to the School Board, advising them of my intention to step down at the end of the current academic year, bringing my long and productive career at Green Meadow High School to a close.

Tracy Flick

Two days after Jack announced his retirement—the news had caught me by surprise, and filled me with a cautious sense of elation—Kyle Dorfman invited me out for a drink at Kenny O.'s Bistropub and Tavern. Normally I would've declined—I tried to avoid mixing work and after-hours socializing—but Kyle was the newly elected President of the School Board, and I needed him in my corner.

People make fun of Mike Pence for refusing to dine alone with women who aren't his wife, but he's not completely wrong. There's always something a little date-like about a man and a woman meeting in a restaurant at night, no matter how much they'd like to pretend otherwise. I was wearing a simple summer dress with a light cardigan over it—very understated—but I could feel Kyle checking me out as I took my seat, dispensing a subtle nod of approval.

"Dr. Flick," he said. "You're looking lovely tonight."

"Thanks," I said. "You're looking well yourself."

Kyle wasn't especially handsome—he was balding and a little bug-eyed—but he kept himself in good shape, and radiated a relaxed but unmistakable aura of self-confidence. It made sense: he was the richest person in Green Meadow, a tech nerd who'd made a fortune in Silicon Valley and then returned to his hometown in New Jersey, where he'd built a ridiculous mansion on the site of his family's old ranch house, and then thrown himself into local politics.

We made a few stabs at small talk, but our hearts weren't in it. As soon as the drinks arrived, we went straight to the main item on the agenda.

"To Principal Weede," I said. "He'll be missed."

"Good Old Jack." Kyle touched his bourbon to my margarita. "May he enjoy his retirement to the fullest."

We drank to Good Old Jack, and then he offered a second toast.

"To Tracy Flick, the next Principal of Green Meadow High School."

"From your lips to the Superintendent's ears," I said.

He waved lazily at the air, as if the Superintendent were a minor nuisance, beneath our consideration.

"Don't worry about Buzz. He doesn't wipe his ass without permission from the Board."

I grimaced in spite of myself. Buzz—Superintendent Bramwell—was a pudgy older man who was always impeccably dressed. I didn't want to visualize him with his pants down.

"Sorry," he said. "I meant that metaphorically. I'm sure his hygiene is beyond reproach."

I was feeling a little agitated, so I took a sip of my drink and glanced around the restaurant, stealing a moment to re-center myself.

"You're going to have to do a search, though, right? Interview some other candidates?"

"Pure formality," he assured me. "As far as I'm concerned, the job is yours. You've earned it."

I felt a smile coming on, but I kept it in check. It's not a good idea to let people see how badly you want something.

"Okay," I said. "I hope it works out that way. I've been getting some feelers from other districts, so . . ."

He nodded vaguely, the way men do when they're no longer paying attention.

"Listen, Tracy. There's something I'd like to run by you. Something I could use your help on."

Kyle Dorfman

When I call myself a visionary, I don't mean that in a grandiose way. I just mean that my best ideas arrive as visualizations rather than abstract concepts. For example, *Barky* came to me in a dream. The whole interface was right there on a phone screen the size of a highway billboard (it was an actual billboard in the dream, glowing fiery red around the edges). Luckily something woke me—probably my own excitement—and I was able to make a quick sketch on the notepad I kept on my nightstand before drifting back to sleep. The rest, as they say, is history.

I wasn't sure how much Tracy knew about me, so I gave her the thumbnail history: Grew up in Green Meadow, graduated high school in 1998, headed to the Bay Area for college (UC Berkeley), and stuck around to become an entrepreneur. I had a few failures and one big success, but I grew disenchanted with the false promises of digital technology and social networking. It wasn't bringing us together; it was making us lonelier and more selfish, less connected to our flesh-and-blood neighbors. I came home because I loved growing up in Green Meadow and wanted my boys to have that same experience. I swear, it was like Mayberry back then, an idyllic little community where people looked out for one another and kids were allowed to be kids without adults breathing down their necks all the time. That freedom made us strong and confident, able to think for ourselves and blaze our own trails in the wider world.

Okay, I know, I'm probably romanticizing it a bit. I do that sometimes. My wife certainly thought so, but Los Gatos wasn't working for her, either, and she was willing to make the change once I agreed to let her design our new house with the architect of her choice (she went with Althea Gruenbaum of Gruenbaum & Vishnu; they had a mind meld in the first five minutes and that was that). The result is bigger and more eye-catching than I would have chosen on my own, but sometimes being in a relationship means making compromises. And I do love the roof deck—it's just me and the treetops and my hot tub up there.

I'm not going to sugarcoat it, though—there was some culture shock. The town looked pretty much the same as it used to, but it felt different. Older. Less vital. More pessimistic about the future. The event that really crystallized it for me was the referendum to finance construction of a new high school. It should have been a no-brainer. The current building was a dump back when I was a kid, and now it's an ancient dump with a leaky roof. The computer lab alone should make every adult in Green Meadow hang their heads in shame. And the gym—it's like that Tenement Museum in Lower Manhattan, where you get to relive the squalor of the past; you can smell adolescent body odor from 1972 hanging in the air. So it was a bitter wake-up call when the votes got tallied and a majority of my fellow citizens said, *Our kids can go to hell. We're fine the way we are.*

Marissa and I thought about moving again, but where would we go? We liked our new house, and the boys were thriving, making friends, riding their bikes all over town, just like I did (except they had better bikes). The only solution that made sense was to stay and fight.

"Tracy," I said. "Have you ever been to Cooperstown?"

"I don't even know where that is."

"Upstate New York. Home of the Baseball Hall of Fame. You should go if you ever get a chance."

She wrinkled her nose. "Not really a fan."

"Me neither," I said. "That's the funny part."

It's my boys who love baseball—they're fierce little jocks, which is a source of constant bemusement to the two computer scientists who created them—and they were the ones who wanted to go. Turns out it's a really cool place. There's this one big room, a literal Hall of Fame, with commemorative plaques celebrating the giants of the game—guys with names like Enos Slaughter and Honus Wagner and Cool Papa Bell—and lots of smaller exhibits displaying the tools of their trade: bats, jerseys, helmets, catchers' masks, whatever. The sacred relics. You can watch videos of the most amazing plays of all time and listen to the voices of dead heroes. You feel yourself in the presence of greatness, and you know what? It makes you want to be great yourself, or at least better than you currently are.

I'd been President of the School Board for eight months at that point, and it had turned out to be a supremely frustrating job. There's so much inertia in public education, so much resistance to change and creative disruption. All my plans for improving things kept receding into the distance, and it was starting to drive me a little crazy.

I was especially worried about the high school. Our test scores were declining; our sports teams sucked; the spring musicals were unwatchable (trust me on this). We'd suffered a handful of overdose deaths in the past decade and at least two suicides. There was a pall of mediocrity and depression hanging over the place. You could see it in the faces of the students, the way they carried themselves. That feeling of pride I'd taken for granted as a teenager—the knowledge that I was a special person growing up in a special place—was gone. What I'd been searching for, without fully realizing it, was a way to bring that back.

The vision came to me, fully formed, while I was standing in front of the Hank Aaron exhibit, contemplating his Gold Glove. I could see it all so clearly. I closed my eyes, let the details imprint themselves on my memory. And then I said it out loud, more to myself than my family.

"We should do this at the high school."

Tracy Flick

We needed a lot of things at GMHS. A new roof. Merit pay for out-standing instructors. Better textbooks. Smarter test prep. Water foun-tains you can actually drink from. Less meddling from the teachers' union. The list went on and on.

Did we *need* a Hall of Fame? Not really. Did I say that to Kyle? No, I did not. Why would I? I wasn't an idiot. I knew I'd need his support when I took over as Principal, and it made no sense to alien-ate him before I even had the job. In fact, I suspected that if I disa-greed with him in our first face-to-face meeting, I might not even get the job. So yes, I let him talk. I nodded and looked interested and muttered a few harmless words of encouragement.

In my defense, it wasn't a completely crazy idea. Lots of schools have a Hall of Fame. Usually the people who get honored are ath-letes, which only reinforces the existing (very unfair) social hierarchy and excludes a lot of exceptional people who are far more deserving of recognition. I actually liked that part of Kyle's pitch—he said he wanted to focus on "a broad spectrum of excellence," celebrating our former students not just for their athletic prowess, but for their intellectual and artistic achievements, their business acumen, their community service, even their parenting skills.

"We could totally honor someone for being an outstanding stay-at-home mom," he told me, though he didn't articulate the criteria for selecting one stay-at-home mom over another. "I have no prob-lem with that."

Some of his proposals were a little over-the-top—the bronze plaques he wanted to affix to the lockers that had belonged to our famous alums, the brass stars he hoped to embed in the sidewalk leading up to the main entrance (the Green Meadow Walk of Fame), the glass display cases he planned to install throughout the school, containing artifacts belonging to our Honorees—clothing they'd worn, musical instruments they'd played, objects they'd invented, or whatever. Like if someone was an astronaut, he said, maybe we could exhibit their space suit and helmet, not that anyone from Green Meadow had ever gone into space. One of our graduates, Raymond Valdez, had made it into the training program, but he had some issues with claustrophobia that ultimately disqualified him. He still works for NASA, but in a more mundane capacity, probably not the kind of job that would get you inducted into a Hall of Fame.

The point is, I was hearing all this for the first time, and doing my best to keep an open mind. It felt like a brainstorming session, like he was throwing a bunch of crap at the wall to see what would stick. I figured we'd scale back to a reasonable level as we moved forward— *if* we moved forward—because that's what usually happens. You ask for the world and settle for scraps.

"What do you think?" he asked. "Give me your honest opinion."

That's the thing about a can of worms. It doesn't always come with a label on it.

"Kyle," I said. "I think it's a great idea."

- 4 -

Esteban Garcia's house was small and run-down, tucked away on a dead-end side street in a mostly commercial neighborhood. There was a dumpster in the driveway, overflowing with construction debris, and a tricycle lying on the patchy lawn. It was the kind of house people bought when they were young and struggling, trying to get a foothold. Vito had received a seven-figure bonus when he signed with the Dolphins, so he'd skipped this particular stage of life.

He rang the bell and waited, steeling his nerves for possible unpleasantness. He'd apologized to eight people so far, and most of them hadn't been happy to see him, or hear his voice on the phone. Especially the women. It was like they'd been waiting for years for Vito to get back in touch, just so they could tell him what an asshole he'd been back in 1997 or 2008 or 2013, and by the way, thanks for the herpes.

He was just about to ring a second time when a chubby, unshaven guy appeared in the doorway. He had a baby in his arms, and a cloth diaper folded over his shoulder. It took Vito a second to recognize him, because in his mind, Esteban was still eighteen, a young warrior in peak physical condition. It happened a lot: guys went to seed in their late twenties, like there was no point staying in shape if they weren't playing football anymore. Vito didn't know how they could stand it, all that muscle turning to flab.

"Coach." Esteban didn't even try to hide his surprise. "Wow. It's been a minute."

Vito nodded at the baby. "Got a little one, huh?"

Esteban grinned, the proud papa. He was wearing a gray T-shirt and blue work pants spattered with white paint.

25

"This is Raúl. He's the new guy. Marisol's three." Esteban patted the baby's back with his big hand. "What about you? How's the family?"

"Okay." Vito nodded for a little too long. "Yeah, you know. Kids are fine. Summer vacation. All that fun stuff."

The baby made a cooing noise. Esteban kissed him on the top of the head, and hoisted him a little higher on his chest.

"So what's up?" he said. "What brings—"

A woman's voice came from inside the house. "Everything okay out there?"

"All good," Esteban replied. "It's Coach Falcone."

A plump, cheerful-looking woman appeared in the hallway, and Vito recognized her with some surprise as Esteban's high school girlfriend, Nikki. She'd been a cheerleader back then, thinner and sexier, a little wild. Marriage and motherhood had softened her, filled her with milky contentment. That had never happened with Susie, or any of Vito's ex-wives, for that matter.

"Hi, Coach. Nice to see you."

"Hey, Nikki. Cute kid you got there."

"Thank you." She looked just as proud as her husband. "We think we'll keep him."

She held out her arms, and Esteban gave her the baby, who immediately launched himself at his mother's breast, his little mouth wide open.

"Dinnertime," she said, smiling sheepishly at Vito before heading back into the house.

"Sorry about that." Esteban looked a little more like himself now that the baby was gone. "So what's up?"

"Yeah . . . so." Vito locked eyes with him, man-to-man. That was the least you could do. "You remember that game your sophomore year? Against St. John's? When I wouldn't let you ride home on the bus?"

"Oh, shit." Esteban grinned, like they were sharing a good memory. "You were so pissed at me. *You forgot to cover the tight end, so I'm gonna forget to take your lazy ass home!* I thought you were kidding, you know? Just making an empty threat."

Vito nodded. He could see it in his head, Esteban standing alone in the parking lot, helmet in hand, watching in disbelief as the bus drove off without him. He was fifteen years old. Big and strong for his age, but still—fifteen.

"That was wrong," Vito said. "I was responsible for you. I shouldn't have abandoned you like that."

Esteban shrugged, like it was water under the bridge.

"No harm, no foul. My pops came and got me."

"Yeah, but you were just a kid. And it was a mean thing to do. To humiliate you like that in front of the team. I have an anger problem, and it was wrong of me to take it out on you."

"It did feel kinda harsh at the time," Esteban conceded. "But, hey, you know what? I never forgot to cover the tight end again."

"No, you didn't. You turned into a great linebacker, and a good man. I'm proud of you."

"Thanks, Coach. That means a lot." Esteban studied Vito for a moment, like he was trying to figure something out. "You, uh . . . want to come in and have a beer or something?"

"That's okay," Vito told him. "I'll leave you to your family. I just wanted you to know that I'm sorry for what I did. I failed you, and I failed a lot of other people, and I'm gonna try to be a better person in the future."

"Okay." Esteban nodded, still a little off balance. "I appreciate that."

They shook hands and Vito headed down the steps and out to the street. He got in his car and shut his eyes for a few seconds. When he opened them, he felt a little better, a little lighter in his soul. He reached for the clipboard on the passenger seat and crossed one more name off the list.

- 5 -

Tracy Flick

The beginning of the school year was always a shock to the system, a headlong plunge into an icy pool. A lot of my colleagues couldn't stop whining about the end of summer, begging for one more week on the beach, one last cookout at the lake house. I pretended to agree, but I was secretly glad to be back in my element, reinhabiting my professional self, the only one that felt truly real to me. I've never been a big fan of vacations.

A lot of my job was routine and bureaucratic, but September was always loose and chaotic, mostly in a good way. The hallways were filled with fresh faces and a manic air of possibility; the whole social order had been reshuffled. New fires kept popping up, and I was the person with the extinguisher. That had always been the case, but it was doubly true now that Jack had announced his retirement. I wanted people to see Tracy Flick taking charge, solving problems, acting as the incumbent.

There were the usual scheduling mishaps, the calls from irate parents who wanted their kids switched to a higher-level class, or an easier class, or the exact same class with a different instructor. I fielded questions about peanut allergies and bus routes and locker assignments, checked in with new teachers to see how they were holding up, and offered tough love to kids who'd gotten cut from the varsity. There were conferences about IEPs, unfounded rumors about all-gender restrooms, and the inevitable complaints about the cafeteria food, along with unhelpful suggestions for how to improve it. Our hapless football coach, Skippy Martino, was upset about the strict new concussion protocol, claiming that two of his best players had been unnecessarily sidelined during the second half of our season opener, leading to a narrow defeat in a game we should have won. I'd chaired the task force that had designed the new protocol, so Skippy didn't get a lot of sympathy from me.

The one problem I didn't see coming was Bridget Dean's nipples. Bridget was a tenured biology teacher, one of the mainstays of our somewhat shaky Science Department. The kids didn't love her—they complained about her voice, a hypnotic monotone that made them want to lay their heads on their desks and drift away—but no one had ever questioned her competence, not even last spring, when she'd handled a difficult divorce like a true professional.

Though only in her midthirties, Bridget had always seemed a little matronly—mousy hair, frumpy clothes, unfashionable eyewear—but she'd transformed herself over the summer. She'd come back blond and twenty pounds lighter, with whiter teeth, better posture, and an unfamiliar bounce in her step. The glasses were gone, and she'd bought herself a whole new wardrobe to highlight her tanned and toned yoga body. All that would have been fine—teachers were people too, as we liked to say—if not for the nipple situation. She wore a bra, but for some reason her nipples were always disconcertingly visible through the fabric of whatever blouse or dress she had on, which had not been the case in the past. Everybody noticed. You could track the disturbance as she walked down the hall—the raised eyebrows, the sidelong glances, the smirks of amusement and boyish arousal. I could only imagine what was happening in her classroom.

Jack let a week go by before raising the subject.

"Excuse me, Tracy." He stood in the doorway and cycled through a series of apologetic expressions, the way he always did before delegating an unpleasant task. "Could you maybe have a word with Bridget? About the, uh . . . dress code?"

"There's not a dress code for teachers," I reminded him. "It's just *appropriate professional attire.*"

"Correct." He wasn't interested in the technicalities. "Just tell her to maybe . . . tone it down a bit, would you?"

"It's kind of a delicate subject."

Jack nodded; he was well aware of this. Avoiding trouble was his superpower.

"I'm sure you'll be very diplomatic," he told me.

Jack Weede

My hands were tied. There was no way that a sixtysomething male administrator could broach the topic of *your erect nipples* with a thirtysomething female teacher and not expose himself to a humiliating lawsuit, along with a virtual stoning on the internet. I had no intention of jeopardizing my hard-earned reputation—not to mention my retirement benefits—in the final lap of my long career.

I know I can sound paranoid about this stuff, but I don't think I'm exaggerating. The pendulum has swung so far in the past few years, I'm amazed I haven't been run out of town on a rail, like so many of my contemporaries. Guys like me are the old guard; we're presumed guilty whether we've done anything wrong or not, though many of us have sinned, I'm not denying it. It's like the French Revolution. They had a just cause, but they got a little overzealous with the guillotine. That's where we are now with all this Me Too business. The-old-guy's-head-in-a-basket phase.

It was such a different world when I started teaching back in 1974. People forget how different. Kids smoked in the bathrooms; fragrant Marlboro clouds wafted out whenever someone opened the door. The boys had fistfights on a regular basis; their friends would gather in a circle and cheer them on. The gay kids got taunted mercilessly—not that anyone admitted to being gay, but bullies made assumptions—and it wasn't uncommon to hear racial slurs in the hallway. Girls got rated on a scale of one to ten; boys would call out their numbers as they passed. Teachers rarely intervened when this stuff happened, because it happened all the time. That was just the way it was, kids being kids, the world being the world. Part of growing up was learning how to handle adversity on your own.

When you're starting out in a career, you take your cues from the people above you. And back in the seventies, the message I got from the older male teachers was pretty clear: the girls were fair game. At my first job in Hillsdale, half the gym teachers were married to their former students. The head of the Math Department, Bart Martinson, was obsessed with a girl in his trig class, a sophomore with an amazing body. He bragged about making her his "assistant." Every day she had to stand in front of the class and write equations on the board.

"She's got a perfect ass," he said. "I want to enjoy the view."

My friend Lou Gardner and I weren't the worst, but we weren't saints, either. We liked to go out drinking on Friday nights, and we always ended up talking about the girls we taught. Who had the best tits, the nicest legs, the sexiest mouth. Who was still a virgin and who was not, who would give the best blowjob, etc. We were young and horny, only a few years out of college, and the Sexual Revolution was in full swing. Our dads were uptight, not us. In 1977, I actually taught *Lolita* to my Honors English class, and instructed my students to think twice before passing judgment on Humbert, maybe take a moment to see the world from his point of view.

No one complained.

I try not to think too much about those days now—let the past be past. The truth is, we're all prisoners of our historical context. Anybody who says morality is absolute, that right and wrong don't change over time, you know what?

They just haven't lived long enough.

Tracy Flick

Bridget was wary at first, and I couldn't blame her. It's not every day a veteran teacher gets summoned to the Assistant Principal's office.

"Is everything okay?" she asked.

"Absolutely," I said. "Just doing a little temperature check. See how things are going."

"Oh." She pressed her palm against her forehead and held it there for a few seconds before giving a cheerful shrug. "Ninety-eight point six."

"Excellent." I nodded as if that was that. "How's everything else? You have a good summer?"

Her body relaxed and her eyes got big.

"Oh my God, Tracy. It was so good. I can't even tell you."

I hadn't been in close quarters with Bridget since school had started, and I found her presence more unsettling than I'd expected. It wasn't that she'd been unattractive in the past. She'd just been a little dull, easy to overlook. But now she was glowing. And it wasn't just the new hairdo or the smoky eyes or the perky nipples. It felt deeper than that, as if she'd undergone a profound inner transformation as well.

"You seem really different," I said.

"I'm happy," she declared, as if it were as simple as that. "I should thank my ex for leaving me. That was the wake-up call I needed."

"Good for you," I said.

"Tracy?" Bridget was peering at me with a hopeful expression. "Do you ever go out dancing?"

"Me? No. Not for a long time."

She leaned forward. Her eyes were bright blue, the same color as her blouse, which was sleeveless and a little tight.

Don't look at her nipples.

"You should come out with me sometime," she said. "There's this club in Lakeview that has a nineties night. Great DJ. Nice crowd. I think you'd like it."

"Sounds fun. But it's not really my thing."

"Okay. No worries. Just thought I'd put it out there."

We traded awkward smiles, the way you do when the small talk has run its course. I let the silence linger for a moment.

"Bridget," I said. "Is it cold in here?"

At first she didn't understand, and then she did.

"Oh my God." Her face had turned an insulted shade of pink. "You've got a lot of nerve."

"Sorry." I gave her a sympathetic smile so she'd know it was nothing personal. "I'm just the messenger."

Jack Weede

I never slept with a student, but there was one time when I cut it pretty close. This happened way back in 1979, my last year at Hillsdale. I was twenty-nine years old, and for the first and only time in my life, I felt like a rock star. I'd always been tall and scrawny, but I'd started lifting weights and had finally grown into my adult body. I'd also cut my hair—I'd been sporting a shaggy, blow-dried look that hadn't been doing me any favors—and I remember being startled by all the compliments I got from my female students.

Nice haircut, Mr. Weede!

Looking good, Mr. Weede!

Take me to the prom, Mr. Weede!

All this was right out in the open—harmless, good-natured flirting that made me blush and stammer, which I guess was the whole point, and did wonders for my self-esteem. Feeling sexually attractive is a powerful drug, especially if you're not used to it.

My flirtation with Mindy DeSantos was different: it was furtive and private, and it felt illicit from the start. Technically speaking, she wasn't one of my students—I'd never taught her in a class, never given her a grade. I was Faculty Advisor for *The Sapling*, the school literary magazine, and Mindy was the Editor, which meant that we spent a lot of time together after school. When no one else was around, she called me by my first name, though not because I gave her permission. She just started doing it one day, and I didn't tell her to stop.

If anything, she was *my* teacher. Mindy was an accomplished singer-songwriter with a lovely voice; she won the schoolwide talent show two years running, and appeared regularly at local open mics. I

36

was a novice guitar player at the time—not much better now, sad to say—and she took it upon herself to help me out. After our editorial meetings, when everyone else had gone home, she took her acoustic guitar out of its case and showed me the chords to Neil Young and Bob Dylan tunes, along with the strumming patterns.

"Down, down, up-down-up," she'd say, encircling my wrist with her fingers, moving my hand to the beat. "There you go. Just like that."

Mindy wasn't especially pretty, wasn't one of the girls Lou and I speculated about on Friday nights. She had a sweet round face; her dark hair was frizzy and a little wild. But it wasn't really about her looks; there was just this current running between us, a really strong connection. Her absence always felt abrupt and unfair when we parted at the end of the day, like somebody had unplugged the radio in the middle of a good song.

And then one afternoon that spring—we'd just put *The Sapling* to bed—she matter-of-factly informed me that her parents were going away for a long weekend to celebrate their anniversary. We were standing in the hallway, not far from the main exit.

"If you're not busy, maybe you could come hang out with me."

I was so startled, I laughed out loud.

"Hang out with you?"

"Yeah." Her face was completely serious. "Bring your guitar. We could jam a little."

"Mindy." I lowered my voice to a whisper. "I can't come to your house."

"It's okay." She put her hand on my arm. "I won't tell anyone."

I jerked my arm away, more forcefully than I meant to.

"Please don't touch me." The hallway was empty, but I felt exposed and vulnerable. "Not in here."

She hung her head for a moment. There were tears in her eyes when she looked up.

"You're such an asshole," she said. Then she turned and walked away, the guitar case banging against her leg.

Mindy was cold to me for the rest of the semester. She started calling me Mr. Weede again, in an overly formal voice, and ignored me at the *Sapling* publication party. She didn't even say goodbye on the last day of school. I was sad that I'd missed my chance with her, but I knew I'd dodged a bullet.

I did run into her at graduation, in the happy chaos after the ceremony. I was wandering through the crowd on the football field, searching for students to congratulate, when I heard a familiar voice.

"Mr. Weede! Over here!"

She smiled when I spotted her, as if all was forgiven, and beckoned me to meet her parents. They were a mismatched pair—the father big and swarthy, the mother wan and petite—but somehow Mindy looked like both of them.

"It's so nice to finally meet you," her mother said. "You did such a terrific job with the magazine."

"Your daughter did all the work," I said. "I just take the credit."

"She talks about you all the time," her father told me. "Mr. Weede this, Mr. Weede that. You made a big impression."

"She's a great kid," I said. "I'm really gonna miss her."

Mindy was blushing, her mortarboard slightly askew.

"I'm gonna miss you too." Her voice broke a little. "Thanks for everything."

We stared at each other. It was still right there, that current humming between us. I've only felt that electricity with one other person in my entire life.

"You're welcome," I said. "Good luck in college."

We hugged for the first time right there on the football field, right in front of her parents. I could feel her body through the flimsy gown, and I didn't want to let go.

Three days later she rang my doorbell at ten in the morning, and I invited her in. There was no reason not to. She was eighteen, a consenting adult, no longer a high school student.

We only had two months together, but they were good ones. She was working as a waitress that summer, covering lunch and dinner shifts, so mornings were our time. I never knew for sure if she was coming over—she liked to surprise me—so most days I just sat around after breakfast, drinking coffee, wondering if she would show up. And then she went off to college, and that was the end of it.

Believe me, I know how shady this sounds. *She came on to me. We waited until she graduated. It was beautiful. No one got hurt.* It's all true, but I would laugh at one of my male teachers if he got caught with a student (even a former student) and tried to make the same excuses.

You're the adult, I would say, right before I fired his sorry ass. *You have all the power. It's up to you to do the right thing.*

For what it's worth, that was the only time I ever crossed the line. I met Alice a few months later, and we've been together ever since. I'm not saying I've been an angel this whole time, or even a very good husband. There were a handful of affairs over the years, but they were always with age-appropriate people, and most of them weren't very serious. All of it stopped the day my wife got sick.

Mindy and I lost track of each other for a while, but we recently reconnected on Facebook. She's in her late fifties now, a married woman with three grown kids. I visit her page sometimes, usually late at night when I'm feeling nostalgic.

There's a photo I like to look at, a black-and-white throwback from the talent show in 1979. Mindy's sitting on a stool, strumming the guitar she used to let me play, her mouth open in the shape of an O. She looks so young and serious in the spotlight, a stray curl falling across her forehead, and I remember how alive I felt on those summer mornings, the agony of waiting and not knowing, the coffee going cold in the mug, and the way my heart jumped when the doorbell rang.

Lily Chu

I was a little early for my meeting with Dr. Flick—she was helping me out with my college essay—so I took a seat in the reception area, right across from Front Desk Diane. That's what everybody called her. It was originally meant to distinguish her from Attendance Lady Diane, who retired when I was a sophomore. It was so people didn't have to say Black Diane and white Diane, which would have been even weirder. Front Desk Diane was the white one.

"How are you, honey?" She called everyone *honey*. "You have a good summer?"

That was a complicated question. Most of my summer had sucked—I was stuck in Green Meadow, working as a lifeguard at the town pool, which sounds okay but was actually incredibly boring.

The end of summer was a lot better, because I went to a two-week code camp in New Hampshire and fell in love with a person named Clem. It was officially a Girls' Code Camp—that was the only reason my parents let me go—but Clem is nonbinary and uses they/them pronouns. We flirted for twelve days and finally hooked up on the last night, both of us feeling stupid for having waited so long, wasting all that precious time. It was an amazing experience, but also really confusing, because I'd always assumed that I was straight, not that I'd had a lot of practice. And now I was back at school, with all kinds of work to do, and absolutely no motivation. All I could think about was Clem. They were a sophomore at Wesleyan, and I had no idea when or if we'd be able to see each other again.

"Pretty good," I said. "How about yours?"

"Quiet." Diane shrugged. "I spent a week at the beach with my sister and her family, but that was about it."

"How's your father?"

"Same." Her face turned sad. "Maybe a little worse."

Front Desk Diane's father had Alzheimer's and lived in a memory care facility. I knew this because we'd done a fair amount of chatting during my junior year, when I had gastrointestinal issues and needed to see the nurse on a semi-regular basis. For some reason they made you check in at the main office first.

"How's your digestion?" she asked.

"Much better," I said. "Knock on wood."

I was about to tell her that I'd taken her advice and gone gluten-free over the summer—she had her own history of stress-related stomach problems—but just then Dr. Flick's door opened and Ms. Dean walked out. She'd lost a lot of weight over the break, and everyone was talking about how hot she was, which was kind of amazing, because she'd been extremely not hot when I'd had her for freshman bio. She passed right by me on her way out.

"Hi, Ms. Dean," I said.

She stopped and squinted, trying to get me in focus. Her face was flushed and she was hugging herself like she was cold, or maybe upset.

"Oh . . . *Lily*," she said, as if I were the one who'd had the makeover. "I didn't even recognize you."

"Did you have a good summer?"

She took a deep breath and released it slowly.

"I did," she said. "But it went by so fast."

- 6 -

Vito felt a vague sense of dread as he touched the digits on his keypad. He'd originally thought it would be easier to make amends over the phone than to do it in person, but it turned out to be the opposite. Face-to-face, people could look in your eyes and see that you were sincere, that you weren't just pretending to be sorry. It was harder over the phone, when all they had was a mental image of the person you used to be.

"Hello?"

"Yes, um . . . is this Kiki?"

There was a brief silence.

"Vito?"

"Yeah. I know it's been a while. I—"

"How did you get this number?"

"I just need a minute, Kiki. I'm—"

"I go by Kimberly now." Her voice was chilly. "And I'm married to a good man, just so you know."

"That's great, Ki . . . Kimberly. I'm happy for you. You deserve that. You were always good to me, and I didn't treat you very well."

"Oh . . ." There was a grudging note of surprise in her voice. "Okay. Huh."

"I'm in recovery," Vito explained. "I'm an alcoholic, and one of the steps—"

"I know the steps." Her voice was softer now. "So you actually want to apologize to me after all these years?"

"I do. From the bottom of my heart. What I did was wrong."

"What did you do?" she coaxed. "I'd like to hear you say it out loud."

"Well, for one thing, I shouldn't have cheated on you."

"Go on. Who'd you cheat on me with?"

"With your cousin, Vanessa."

"She was more than my cousin. She was like my sister and my best friend all in one. I hope it was worth it for you, Vito."

"I'm a selfish person; I always was. I know I can't fix the damage I've done, but I want you to know that I sincerely regret it."

"Well . . ." She made a sound that was half chuckle, half sigh. "That's better than nothing, I guess. I appreciate it."

Vito hesitated. He could've ended the call there, but that would have been a disservice to both of them.

"There's one other thing," he told her. "My mom's not dead."

"*What?*"

"Yeah, she's fine. She lives in North Carolina with my dad. They play a lot of golf."

"Are you fucking kidding me?"

"I'm sorry I lied to you."

"Why would you do that?" She sounded genuinely bewildered. "Why would you say . . ."

"I don't know. I just . . . thought it was gonna be a one-night thing. I didn't think we'd end up in a—"

"Oh my God," she said. "You are a piece of human trash."

"I'm gonna do better from now on," Vito said, but the call was over by then.

- 7 -

Tracy Flick

Kyle's Hall of Fame proposal received unanimous approval from the School Board. To my amazement, he got everything he asked for—the plaques, the display cases, even the stars in the sidewalk—without any scaling back whatsoever. The thing I hadn't understood was that he was funding the whole operation out of his own pocket, through the Dorfman Family Foundation. The Board was more than happy to let him throw his money around.

Our Selection Committee met for the first time in mid-October. There were five of us, three adults—Kyle, Jack, and myself—and two students. This was Kyle's one and only concession to the Board. He'd wanted unilateral decision-making power, but his colleagues had pressed for a more inclusive and transparent process, and Kyle had reluctantly agreed.

As for the students, it made sense to invite Nate Cleary and Lily Chu—the President and Vice President of the Student Council—to serve with us on the Committee. After all, they'd already been chosen by their peers; nobody could accuse us of playing favorites. And they were both impressive kids—Lily more so than Nate, by a wide margin, though of course Nate had won the election.

Lily Chu

We went to a restaurant for our first meeting. A really nice one, right in the middle of the school day. I was sitting next to Principal Weede, and neither of us knew what to say to each other. At one point I mentioned that I couldn't eat gluten, and Mr. Dorfman heard me from across the table.

"Why's that?" he asked. "Do you have celiac disease?"

"Just an allergy, I think. My doctor's not sure."

"What do you mean, he's not sure?"

"*She*," I said. "My doctor's a she. She said the test was ambiguous."

"I bet it was." He laughed like my doctor was a fool. "There's no such thing as a gluten allergy. You either have celiac disease or you don't. And celiac disease is quite rare."

What was I supposed to say? *Well, I used to have diarrhea a lot, but I don't get it so much anymore*?

"They've got some gluten-free dishes that look pretty good," Dr. Flick told me. "You'll be fine."

She gave me a sympathetic smile, very mom-like, which I appreciated. She had a reputation around school for being kind of a bitch, but that wasn't my experience. She'd been really sweet last spring, when I lost the election by twenty-seven votes and had to settle for Veep, which wouldn't look nearly as good on my applications.

The world's not fair, she told me. And then she gave me a big hug and whispered in my ear: *You're better than they are. Don't ever forget that.*

Nate Cleary

I was thrilled to be there, sitting at the same table as Kyle Dorfman. I mean, I have no idea if those net worth numbers on the internet are true—I'm guessing probably not—but even if you chopped that figure in half, you're still talking a shitload of money, and now Kyle and I were hanging out on a Tuesday afternoon, sharing a side order of spicy fries.

On the surface I kept it pretty chill, though. At least I was less weird about it than Lily, who kept blushing and stammering whenever he asked her a question, which was kind of surprising, because she'd always been way more mature than everybody else in our class. I mean, even back in first grade, she used to bring books to the playground and read them at the picnic table during recess, while everyone else ran around screaming like idiots and throwing wood chips in the air.

I did make one minor misstep. It happened in the middle of dessert, when Kyle finally got down to business, and asked us who we wanted to put in the Hall of Fame. I guess I should have waited for the adults to chime in, but I was feeling pretty comfortable by then, and the answer seemed so obvious I just blurted it out.

"It has to be either you or Vito Falcone, right?"

He looked a little startled when I said that, like it had never even occurred to him that he might be in the running.

"Seriously," I said. "Did you ever look at the Green Meadow Wikipedia page? They have this section, like Notable Residents or whatever? And the two top names are Vito Falcone and Kyle Dorfman. After that it's just a bunch of randos no one's ever heard of."

Jack Weede

You know how Kyle got rich?

He designed a virtual pet app called *Barky*. His big innovation—the thing that set his virtual pet app apart from all the other ones—was that the dog barked out its thanks whenever you remembered to feed it or take it for a walk or clean up after it took a virtual shit. For a year or so, millions of people thought that making Barky happy was a rewarding way to kill some time, and then they forgot all about it.

That's his entire claim to fame.

Kyle Dorfman

People like to mock *Barky*, as if it was some stupid fad from the Dark Ages. What they forget is that there was an innovative social component to the app. We called it the Love Bank. If you did a nice thing for Barky, gave him a biscuit or a bath or a bone, you would earn Gratitude Hearts—they would float up from the dog's head and deposit themselves in a treasure chest—and you could use these hearts as currency. You could buy more bones and biscuits, or give them as a birthday gift to a friend, or transfer them to someone you had a crush on, or bestow them on a stranger who asked for help.

That was what people got excited about. Not the cute dog. The fact that the cute dog was at the center of an economy of affection and kindness, a benevolent space where one good deed led to another. And yes, it made me a lot of money. I don't like to say how much, because it's a shocking amount, almost obscene. But the Hall of Fame wasn't about me.

"Just to be clear, I'm not a candidate. It wouldn't be ethical for a member of the Committee." I glanced around the table. "And just for the record, if everybody else wants to go with Vito Falcone, that's totally fine with me. More than fine. I think he'd be an awesome choice."

"It would make a splash," Jack agreed. "But only if you could get him to attend the ceremony. We've tried to bring him back a few times, but he's always *too busy*. No point in honoring a guy who's not gonna show up."

"Do you have his contact info?"

49

"Check with Front Desk Diane. She's probably got something on file."

Lily poked her hand into the air.

"Can I ask a stupid question?" She looked a little embarrassed. "Who's Vito Falcone?"

Nate Cleary

Lily's parents were immigrants—I'm pretty sure they went to high school in Taiwan or someplace like that—so it made sense she'd never heard of him. My dad had grown up right here in Green Meadow, and I'd been hearing his name all my life.

"Vito Falcone was the greatest football player in the history of our town," I told her. "His junior and senior years, the Larks were undefeated and ranked number one in the state."

"That was a long time ago," Principal Weede told her. "You weren't even born yet."

"He only played in the NFL for a couple of years," I said. "But still, nobody from here ever made it that far in any professional sport. Not even close."

"And he was really good-looking." Kyle whipped out his phone and did some swiping. "Movie star handsome. He was like a young god back in the day."

He held up the phone so we could all take a look. It was a picture from Vito's college days at the University of Pittsburgh. He was holding a football by his ear, gazing thoughtfully into the distance, as if he were about to throw downfield.

Tracy Flick

I'd heard his name before, but that was the first time I ever saw his face. That square jaw. Those vapid blue eyes. That bottomless self-confidence. Like he'd never experienced a moment of doubt or loneliness or failure in his entire life. My reaction was immediate and visceral.

Ugh, I thought. *I know that guy.*

From as far back as I could remember, no matter where I went or what I did, there was always a Vito Falcone. The Golden Boy. The Handsome Jock. The Big Man on Campus. Let's laugh at his stupid jokes and tell him how great he is. Let's pay him more than he's worth. Let's give him a promotion. Let's elect him President. Let's put his face on a bronze plaque.

I don't know why it bothered me so much. I honestly didn't care who got inducted into the Hall of Fame. All I wanted was for things to run smoothly, to put on an event that would make people proud of their community and their high school, and reinforce my own image as a competent and trustworthy leader.

I guess I just felt like Kyle had pulled a bait and switch on me. This was nothing like the inspiring vision he'd pitched at Kenny O.'s, the Hall of Fame that would honor musicians and astronauts and public servants and stay-at-home moms. This was just the opposite, the same old crap as always. I was trying to think of a diplomatic way to say so, when Jack raised a different objection.

Jack Weede

Yes, the money was Kyle's, but the high school didn't belong to him, and neither did the Hall of Fame, as much as he would have liked to think otherwise. These were public institutions; they belonged to the community, and the community had a right to be involved. You couldn't just have one backroom meeting and pick the first person who popped into your head. That wasn't democracy.

"The only fair thing," I said, "is to solicit nominations from the public. Let the people tell us who we should honor."

"Then why are we even here?" Kyle said. "What's our role?"

"We're the jury. We'll go through the nominations, draw up a short list, and make the final decision."

"That's a lot of unnecessary work," Kyle muttered. "Especially since we all know it's gonna be Vito."

"Probably," I agreed. "But if that's where we do land, and I agree that there's a very good chance we will, at least people won't feel like we shoved him down their throats. They'll feel like their voices were heard and respected, and the result was legitimate. And if that means the five of us have to put in a little extra work, then so be it."

Tracy Flick

It was a productive first meeting. Thanks to Jack, we came out of it with a clear process and a concrete timetable: nominations in November, short list and final vote in December, event prep in January and February, Induction Ceremony in March. It would be tight, but it looked doable.

At my suggestion, we voted to increase the number of inductees to two. At least that way we'd get a chance to honor one individual who wasn't a star quarterback, the most obvious and depressing choice in the world.

PART TWO:

Be the Flame

- 8 -

Diane Blankenship liked to do her grocery shopping between nine thirty and ten at night, after she was done at the gym, and right before the supermarket closed. It was a little awkward sometimes, wandering through the store in her sweaty workout clothes, but the Pathmark was usually pretty empty at this time of night, and she rarely ran into anyone she knew. All she wanted was a little time to herself, a chance to decompress after another day behind the front desk at GMHS, answering the phones and greeting visitors, doing her best to make everyone feel at home.

That was the big problem with her job, which she otherwise enjoyed, and which she'd been doing for her entire adult life: It was just so *visible*, like she was the public face of the school, its good-will ambassador to the world. People recognized her wherever she went—restaurants, waiting rooms, red lights even, when she was just sitting in her car, minding her own business—almost like she was some kind of weird celebrity. *Hey, Diane!* they'd call out. *Front Desk Diane!* And she would smile and wave and make the effort of small talk because it felt rude not to, and because she had a reputation to uphold.

But it was so much more relaxing to be left alone, to push her cart at her own slow pace up and down the bright aisles, savoring the endorphin afterglow from her elliptical session. Her mind was pleasantly empty, nothing to think about but the piped-in music, song after song she'd completely forgotten about—right now it was "Lyin' Eyes" by the Eagles—though it turned out she always knew the words by heart, and sometimes got a little weepy as they flashed through her mind, not because they meant anything special, but just because they reminded her of the past, the way your life slipped by, day after day, moment after moment, until all the good stuff was behind you.

On the other side of town a boy is waiting . . .

Diane had always had a good memory; everyone said so. *You're just like your father,* her mother used to say. *He never forgets a thing.* But her mother was dead now, and her father barely knew his own name. Half the time he didn't recognize Diane when she visited him after work—though he was always happy to sit and chat for a while—and the other half he mistook her for her mother, and Diane always played along, because it made him so happy.

She didn't need much in the way of groceries, but she took her time, visiting every aisle, "Lyin' Eyes" flowing into "Baker Street," and then into "What's Love Got to Do with It," which was the one that got her choked up, because it was true what Tina Turner said, every last word of it.

She told herself to go straight home—hop in the shower, put on some clean PJs, get a good night's sleep—but that was just for show, a little game she played with herself. There was one quick stop she needed to make on the way, though it wasn't exactly on the way. She'd been going there a lot lately, way too much, and it was beginning to worry her, this feeling of urgency and agitation that had been building up inside of her throughout the fall, a sense that something needed to be done, that the status quo was unacceptable.

It had started the first day of school, when Jack announced his retirement. He didn't give her any advance warning, didn't take her aside and whisper a few kind words to cushion the blow, not that she was surprised. He'd made it painfully clear over the past several years that her emotional needs were no longer part of the equation. She was just another member of his "main office team," and not a very important one at that—just the secretary who answered the phone, the one who'd been there forever. She wasn't surprised by his behavior, only by how much it hurt, how raw the wound still was after the ancient bandage got ripped away.

It took her a week to work up the courage to knock on his door. He looked a little worried when he saw her there—she used to stand in that doorway a lot—but he recovered quickly. He was a master of the quick recovery.

"I'm happy for you," she said. "That's great news about your wife."

"Thank you," he said. "It's quite a relief."

"And you got an RV?"

He looked a little sheepish, because she knew him well enough to know that he wasn't an RV kind of guy.

"It's a Winnebago," he explained. "She wants to take it out west. Visit the national parks."

"That sounds nice," Diane said, and she meant it.

"Well." He glanced at his stapler, then out the window. Anywhere but her face. "She's been through the wringer. She deserves a little . . ."

He couldn't finish the sentence, or didn't want to, so Diane finished it for him in her mind. Alice deserved a little pampering, a little love, some time to enjoy life when she wasn't scared or sick or in pain. Of course she did.

"Anyway." Jack nodded at his computer screen. "I've got some . . ."

"Oh, sure," she said. "No worries. Sorry to bother you."

"Thank you, Diane." He was an old man now, still handsome—Tracy Flick said he looked like a Senator who'd been voted out of office—but his shoulders were stooped, and his face had taken on a hangdog quality, as if his cheeks were beginning to melt. It should have made her feel better somehow, but it didn't. "That's very thoughtful of you."

She returned to the front desk, feeling sick and helpless, and forced her face into its habitual mask of welcome. *Thank you, Diane. That's very thoughtful.* It felt like a poison pill was dissolving in her gut, very slowly, spreading all the way out to her fingers and toes, and that night she drove to his house for the first time in years, just to take a quick look at the famous RV. It was bigger than she'd imagined—very comfortable looking—and of course she'd gone back the next night and the night after that, because that was what she needed right now. To hold a vigil in front of Jack's stupid Winnebago and feel her own pain.

He used to tell her that she was the love of his life—maybe not in those exact words—and she'd believed him, up to a point. She still did, despite all the evidence to the contrary. He said there'd only been one other woman with whom he'd shared such a powerful connection, some college girl—a folk singer—he'd dated for a summer in his twenties. He said he'd never had anything like that with his wife, though they cared deeply for each other and made a good parenting team.

But this, he'd say, meaning the two of them and whatever sex they'd just had. *This is . . . a whole other thing.*

They'd worked together for eight years before anything happened. There'd been some flirting—a hand on an arm, eye contact that lasted a little too long—but it all felt fairly safe and aboveboard. They were both married and he had almost twenty years on her, a whole generation spread out between them.

She caught him looking at her body sometimes, and he always responded with a sweet, guilty shrug, as if he couldn't help himself. He paid a lot of attention to her clothes. *Yellow's a good color for you,* he'd say. She wasn't getting much of that from her husband, that was for sure. Lance was the exact opposite, always a little underwhelmed by whatever she had to offer. *I don't love those jeans,* he'd say. Or: *Something's a little weird about this sauce.* Or: *Jesus, would you watch it with the teeth?*

And then Lance walked out on her right after the holidays, no warning at all, unless you count years of unhappiness as a warning. He said he'd had an epiphany at work, a sudden blinding realization that his life was all wrong. He didn't want to be an accountant anymore, or a husband, and he definitely didn't want to go through another round of IVF with her.

I'm suffocating, he said. *I need a new adventure.*

Me too, she told him. *Let's do it together.*

Diane, he said with a weary sigh. *That would defeat the purpose.*

Jack got a lot more attentive after her divorce. He started taking her out to lunch, and then they graduated to drinks after work. He let her cry on his shoulder, gave a lot of emotional support at a time when she really needed it.

Lance made a big mistake, he told her one night. *What the hell was he thinking?*

That I'm boring. He says I've never done an interesting thing in my life.

Jack was indignant on her behalf, and she loved him for that.

You are not boring, he assured her. *And Lance is a jackass, if you ask me.*

He could've kissed her that night—could've fucked her in the back seat of his car if he'd wanted to—but he didn't even try. He took his time, made her work. She started dressing for him, choosing outfits that were a little sexier than before, that would make him pay attention. She'd present herself to him in the mornings, standing silently in his doorway, letting him drink her in.

What am I gonna do with you? he'd ask. *How am I supposed to concentrate?*

He only disapproved once, the day she showed up in a leather skirt and stilettos, a bold statement for the main office. The skirt was a little slutty—really tight across the hips and ass—and he didn't even try to hide his disappointment.

This is a school, he told her. *Not a night club.*

She was embarrassed and apologetic; the whole day felt like an endless walk of shame. The next morning she toned it way down, loose gray pants and a baggy maroon sweater. Flat shoes. That was the day he called to her as she was heading out for lunch.

Excuse me, Diane. Do you have a minute?

She went to his doorway, feeling suddenly shy.

Why don't you come in. His voice was soft, almost melancholy. *You can lock the door if you want.*

Sometimes he came to her apartment, but most of their relationship happened in his office. He liked fucking her in there, bending her over the armrest of the couch, pulling her panties to one side, or spicing up a dull workday with an under-the-desk blowjob (he never complained about her teeth). Usually they waited until late afternoon, when the main office had emptied out—Attendance Lady Diane left at three back then so she could be home with her kids after school, and Larry Holleran, the Assistant Principal at the time, was still coaching football and wrestling, a ridiculous arrangement—but every so often they risked it in the middle of the day. It made her feel cheap sometimes, and a little paranoid—she was sure everyone knew what they were up to, that they could smell it on her—but she loved having a secret, something that only belonged to her and Jack. She wished Lance could see her in the Principal's office—he was living in Alaska by then, working on a fishing boat—and understand just how badly he'd misjudged her.

This is me, she'd think, imagining her ex-husband's shock as she straddled her boss on his Aeron chair. *This is my adventure.*

They managed it for two years without getting caught, though there were a few close calls. And then one day—it felt like a lifetime ago—Jack got to school three hours late, looking dazed and ashen, unsteady on his feet.

Diane, he said. *I need a word with you.*

He said that sometimes when he wanted to fuck her—*I need a word with you*—but this wasn't that. She followed him into his office and sat down beside him on the couch. He ran his hand slowly through his hair, pushing upward.

Alice has cancer, he said. *It's bad. Really bad.*

Then he burst into tears, which was something she'd never seen before. She held him and shushed him and kissed the top of his head, and those were the last kisses she ever gave him.

The Weedes lived in the hilltop section of Poplar Ridge, in a solid-looking colonial with a portico, a sunporch, and a sloping front lawn. Diane parked in her usual spot across the street, in the shadowy no-man's-land between two McMansions that hadn't been there nine years ago, the last time she visited this neighborhood at night, in that strange uncertain period after Alice got sick. Jack couldn't have been too happy about the new neighbors, whose houses were so much bigger and more ostentatious than his own. That was the kind of thing that drove him crazy, people flaunting their wealth, five bedrooms and seven baths, three luxury SUVs in the cobblestone driveway.

There were two lights on inside his house, one upstairs and one down, the usual configuration. She imagined Alice up in bed, reading under the covers—apparently she was a big reader—and Jack down in the living room, dozing off in front of Rachel Maddow. She wondered if they even slept in the same bedroom anymore. So many older couples didn't, usually because the man snored too much, though she had no idea if Jack was a snorer. She'd never spent a night with him, and that was something she regretted. It was such a simple pleasure, rolling over and opening your eyes, finding someone there who was happy to see you.

A car went by, moving slowly. She resisted the urge to duck down in her seat, to pretend she wasn't there. There was nothing illegal about parking on a public road, staring out the window at your ex-lover's house, at the life that could've been your own.

Because it really had felt that way, at least in the beginning. *Terminal,* Jack had told her. *Six months to a year.* He didn't say a word about the future, about what might be possible in a world without Alice, but Diane couldn't help filling in the blanks. Of course they put their affair on hold; the poor woman was dying.

But Alice didn't die. She held on for nine years—surgery, chemo, more surgery, more chemo, experimental treatments, on and on—and now she was cured. It was a miracle, everyone said so, and Diane always agreed, because it was the only thing a decent person could do.

- 9 -

Tracy Flick

I got up early on Saturday morning and baked a carrot cake for my daughter's eleventh birthday. I took my time with it, spreading out on the kitchen counter, giving each task my full attention— grating the carrots, chopping the walnuts, blending the frosting with the ancient, hand-cranked eggbeater I'd inherited from my mother. I thought about her every time I used it, the way we would bake together on the weekends, especially if one of us was feeling down.

Let's make some cupcakes, she'd say. *Beats moping, right?*

Sophia wasn't around to help, which was too bad. She was at her father's house, and I would be joining them for dinner later in the day, after I made an appearance at the football game. Jack Weede had made a point of attending every Larks home game for the past twenty years—*So many ruined Saturdays,* he liked to brag—and it seemed like something I should start doing now that I was campaigning for the top job, despite my lifelong hatred of football and the culture that went along with it. If it was up to me, I'd eliminate the entire sport, though I knew better than to say that out loud.

Daniel and I had a week-on, week-off custody arrangement. It was an amicable situation that worked well for everyone, and created the defining rhythm of my life. I enjoyed my daughter's company, but I savored the child-free interludes as well, when I didn't have to cook real meals or pretend to care about *The Bachelor,* and could

65

work or read or meditate in the evenings without interruption. My sex life, such as it was—infrequent "movie nights" with a widowed surgeon who was getting a little clingy—took place entirely during the weeks Sophia spent with Daniel and his wife, Margaret, and their chubby yellow Lab, Boomer.

But even if it had been my week, I doubt Sophia would have been helping out in the kitchen. We weren't the kind of mother and daughter who baked together, or played board games, or went to garage sales on weekend mornings. To be honest, we just weren't that close, at least not in the exclusive way I'd been with my own mother—the two of us against the world, so deeply connected it was hard to tell where one of us left off and the other began.

Maybe it would have been different if I'd raised her on my own, put a little more of my stamp on her. Maybe then we would have been a team—the Flick girls, an inseparable duo, sharing the same hopes, dreams, and heartbreaks. But Sophia was her father's daughter too, and that had made all the difference. Like Daniel, she was sunny and easygoing, uncompetitive, a little lazy. She liked to sing and dance, but had no interest in taking lessons. She enjoyed sports, but didn't care if she was on the A team. It had never once occurred to her that she needed to be the best, or had to prove herself to anyone, and we had no trouble figuring out where one of us left off and the other began.

Daniel was my grad school professor, a middle-aged man with a little potbelly, a dry sense of humor, and a full head of thick, silver-gray hair. He was smart and provocative, a self-proclaimed "progressive educator" who wanted to eliminate grades, abolish standardized testing, and make college tuition free for everyone. I was an AP History and Government teacher at Grover Regional, an outspoken critic of grade inflation, and an advocate for a more rigorous, back-to-basics curriculum. Daniel and I got into a lot of arguments, some of which continued long after class let out, until our cars were the only two left in the parking lot.

It wasn't much of an affair. A couple of coffee dates, a fancy dinner, and one rainy weekend at an inn in Vermont, where we had pretty good sex in a very nice bed, but ended up in a prolonged dispute about Rudolf Steiner that consumed the rest of our stay and the entire drive home, at the end of which Daniel informed me that I was *exhausting* and *relentless*, and that he didn't think we should see each other anymore, and I said that was fine with me.

If not for Sophia, inadvertently conceived before we drifted onto the topic of Waldorf Schools, I would have been a minor chapter in Daniel's midlife crisis. He'd thought he wanted something different—a younger woman, a new beginning—but the time he spent with me helped him realize that his marriage was worth saving, so I guess he has two things to thank me for.

I was doing some tricky work with the piping bag when my landline rang.

"Call from . . . *Dr. Kinder*," said the female robot on my answering machine. "Call from . . . *Dr. Kinder*."

Ugh.

Dr. Kinder was Philip, the man I'd been seeing for the past two years, and avoiding for the past two weeks.

"Tracy," he said, after the beep. "Sorry to bother you on your landline. I tried your cell again, but you didn't pick up and I . . . Look, we really have to make a decision about Thanksgiving. My sister needs a head count."

I liked Philip, I really did. He was smart and charming and kept himself in excellent shape for a man in his late fifties (we'd met at a 10K charity road race for cystic fibrosis, both of us running at the exact same pace). He was well-known and widely admired in Green Meadow—an orthopedic surgeon who had raised three kids on his own, after his wife had died of breast cancer—and I was a little annoyed by the surprise some people (some *women*, to be precise) expressed when they learned that we were dating.

Wow, they'd say, examining me a little more closely, as if maybe they'd missed something. *Lucky you!*

Lucky him, I always wanted to say, though I never did.

Philip was my first real boyfriend in ages, and the only one in my entire life who'd lasted more than a year.

Things were fine between us—light and casual—until this past summer, when he started pushing in a more serious direction, inviting me on double dates with his married friends, trying to interest me in romantic weekend getaways to Hilton Head or Nantucket, and then getting upset when I said no, or canceled at the last minute.

I want to spend more time with you, he said. *Is that so crazy?*

I didn't know what to tell him. I always looked forward to our movie nights. I liked snuggling with him on the couch, and I liked having sex with him, but the minute we were done, I just wanted him to get dressed and go home. I didn't want to cuddle and whisper in the dark, and I didn't want him to sleep over. We'd tried that once, at his insistence, and I'd hated it, waking to the dead weight of his arm on my chest, the awkwardness of morning conversation.

"Okay," he sighed. "Could you please call me back, Tracy? We need to make a decision."

By the time I realized I was pregnant, Daniel and I were out of touch. I was all set to get an abortion—I didn't think I had a choice, a single woman with a full-time job and a dissertation to write—but my mother begged me to reconsider. Her health wasn't good, and she was worried about what would become of me when she was gone and I was alone in the world.

You'll love your child, she told me. *You won't believe how much.*

I decided to go through with it, as much for her sake as my own, though I'm not sure I admitted that to myself at the time. I thought having a grandchild might extend my mother's life, keep her tethered to the world a little while longer. At the very least, I knew it would give her some joy, which had been in short supply for a long time.

Oh, honey, she told me. *You won't regret it. Not for a minute.*

I didn't want to tell Daniel, but again my mother disagreed. She'd always felt guilty about being a single parent, chronically short on money and time. She thought Daniel should be held accountable—made to pay his fair share—and believed my daughter would benefit from the presence of a positive male role model; she said it might save her from a lifetime of searching for father figures and mistaking them for romantic partners. It was hard for me to argue with that.

I thought Daniel would be upset by the news—he was already reconciled with Margaret at that point—but he surprised me. There were no recriminations, not even a trace of hesitation. He said of course he'd pay child support, and do whatever he could to help. He had only one condition—that he be allowed to visit his daughter and have a relationship with her.

She's mine too, he said. *I'd love to get to know her.*

I was grudging at first, but single motherhood was hard, and child care insanely expensive. And then my own mother died—Sophia was only eight months old—and it was such a godsend to be able to hand the baby over to Daniel when I needed some time to myself. Margaret helped a lot too. She fell in love with Sophia, and she was always kind to me, as if I'd never done a thing to hurt her.

The football game was as tedious as I expected. I spent most of it sitting behind the Booster Club merch table with Ricky Pizzoli, selling T-shirts and bumper stickers that said *Go Larks!* and *Proud Lark Parent* and *I Love My Lady Lark.* Ricky was a local landscaping magnate, a big man with a white mustache who severely overestimated his own charm. Unfortunately, he was also on the School Board, so I did my best to look interested while he ranted about the humiliating decline of our football program—we were having another terrible season—and the excruciating incompetence of our coach, Skippy Martino. Ricky was a former GMHS football player himself, a proud veteran of the Golden Age, back when Larry Holleran was Head Coach, and Green Meadow was one of the best teams in the state.

"You remember Larry, right?"

"Sure," I said. "I took over for him when he left."

Ricky looked puzzled for a moment, but then he did the math.

"That's right, I forgot he was Assistant Principal. He was always just Coach Holleran to me." His face got a little dreamy. "I'm telling you, Tracy, he was the most inspiring man I ever knew. Kind of a Vince Lombardi type. No excuses, that was his whole philosophy. You keep your mouth shut and you execute the plan and you win games. It's not that complicated." He glared at me, as if I'd suggested that it was, and then heaved a wistful sigh. "Man, I wish we could get him back here. He'd turn this ship around pretty fast, I'll tell you that."

"Maybe so," I said, though it wasn't very likely. Larry Holleran had left Green Meadow to coach football at a small college in western Pennsylvania, and according to Jack he was loving every minute of it.

"What can you do, though?" Ricky said. "You can't blame an outstanding guy like that for moving on to bigger and better things."

"No." I forced a smile. "I guess you can't."

Still, I was glad I went. A lot of people stopped by the table to say hi and shake my hand, students and alums and parents alike, and they all seemed happy to see me. I chatted briefly with Mayor Milotis, and also with Charisse Turner, the only Black member of the School Board. Jack Weede gave me a thumbs-up, and Kyle Dorfman introduced me to his wife, Marissa.

"Oh, wow," she said. "The famous Tracy Flick. It's so nice to finally meet you. You're a lot younger than I thought."

She was wearing a long, belted sweater, and her hair was blowing charmingly across her face. I felt a little self-conscious in my oversized GMHS hoodie and no-nonsense ponytail.

"I'm not that young," I said. "But thank you."

"Well, you look it," she assured me. "That's just as good."

Kyle and Ricky launched into a jargon-filled analysis of the game, cursing Skippy's inept defensive strategy, which apparently had something to do with his use of a three-four in situations that called for a four-three, and vice versa. I was glad to see that Marissa was as bored by this as I was. Kyle flashed me a knowing smile.

"Guess you're not much of a football fan, huh, Tracy?"

"Oh no," I said quickly. "I love all the sports. It's just, I'm more of a soccer mom. My daughter plays on Saturdays, so . . . "

"Good for her." Kyle nodded at his wife. "Marissa was a soccer player. Varsity midfielder at Pomona."

"Center mid," she added, as if this was an important distinction. "But I quit after sophomore year. It was a huge time commitment."

"Huh." Ricky gave her a once-over that was more detailed than it needed to be. "I can see that. You've got those nice long legs."

Kyle turned to me. "What about you, Tracy. What sport did you play?"

I hesitated. This was a bit of a sore subject, the only gap in my youthful résumé.

"I wasn't much of an athlete," I said. "I did everything else. Clubs and drama and yearbook and Model UN and the school paper. Student Government. That was my big thing."

"That makes sense." Ricky smirked, as if he'd suspected as much. "I bet you were President of your class."

I stiffened a little, the way I always do when men speak to me in a condescending tone.

"The whole school," I told him. "I was President of Everything."

I didn't mean it as a joke, but they all laughed, even Marissa. It must have been the way I said it.

"I ran a few marathons in my early thirties," I added so they'd know I wasn't a complete couch potato.

"Boston?" Kyle asked.

"Just New York. And the one up in Newport. I did that twice."

"Damn, girl." Marissa offered her fist and I gave it a bump. "That's pretty badass."

"What about you?" I asked Kyle. "What did you play?"

He shrugged, like sports weren't really his thing, either. "Just intramural Ultimate for a couple of years, when I was an undergrad." He paused, then broke into a sheepish grin. "And not to brag, but I was also three-time Ping-Pong champ of my frat."

Ricky smirked. "You were in a frat?"

"The nerd frat," Marissa explained.

"Maybe so," Kyle admitted. "But those tournaments were intense."

"I used to be pretty good at Ping-Pong," I said.

"Huh." Kyle studied me with fresh interest. "Maybe we should play sometime."

"Fine with me."

Ricky glanced at Marissa. "My money's on Tracy."

"Mine too," she said.

"You guys are betting on the wrong horse." Kyle slashed an imaginary paddle through the air. "I've got a wicked serve. She'll be lucky to score five points."

"You never know," I said. "I might surprise you."

"Nah." He grinned and looked me straight in the eye. "I'll crush you, Tracy."

"Oh my God," Marissa groaned. "I'm married to a seventh grader."

A big cheer erupted from the visitors' side of the stadium. Ricky and Kyle winced in unison.

"You know what our problem is?" Ricky observed. "We have a loser mentality. That's what Larry Holleran used to say. Losers go out on the field expecting to lose, and they make sure that happens." He shook his head in disgust. "They're just fulfilling their own destiny."

Sophia and her friend Izzy greeted me at the door, both of them in their red-and-white soccer uniforms, made festive by the addition of Mardi Gras beads. Boomer followed close behind, panting heavily, his entire back end wiggling in frantic welcome, as if it were about to break loose from the rest of his body. I wasn't crazy about dogs—they seemed unclean to me, and a little pathetic—but Sophia loved Boomer so much I felt obliged to show him some affection. Unaware of my bad faith, he gazed up at me with moist, adoring eyes as I knelt and scratched his neck.

"How'd the game go?" I asked.

"We tied," Sophia said. "Two to two."

"Tied?" I averted my face to avoid the dog's revolting breath. "Don't they have an overtime or something?"

Izzy shook her head. "We just play the two halves. When it's over, it's over."

"Huh." Despite what I'd told Kyle at the stadium, I wasn't much of a soccer mom. Daniel loved watching Sophia's games, and I always had a lot of work on the weekends, so I was happy to delegate. "That can't be very satisfying."

"It's fine," Sophia said with a shrug. "Nobody loses."

It was the usual scenario in the kitchen, Margaret bustling around while Daniel relaxed at the counter, sipping wine, bobbing his head to Salsa music on the Sonos. He'd spent a year in Nicaragua in the eighties and did his best to keep in touch with Latino culture.

"Look who's here," he said. "And she even baked a cake."

I lifted the cover of the cake dish to display my handiwork. I'd added my own little flourish—six tiny carrots made of orange and green frosting, spaced evenly around the perimeter.

"Mom, wow." Sophia stroked my arm. "I love it."

I kissed the top of her head. "Happy birthday, sweetie."

"It's adorable," Margaret added, lifting the hem of her apron to dab at some perspiration on her brow. "You really went the extra mile."

The girls excused themselves, disappearing into Sophia's room to watch videos and giggle together until dinner was served. They'd been best friends since preschool, and as far as I could tell, had never had an argument. All they ever did was agree, breathlessly, and with great enthusiasm. I was a little jealous; I'd never had a friend like that.

Daniel handed me a glass of wine. He was sixty-four, and quite a bit heavier than when we'd first met, but he still had that beautiful silver hair.

"Eleven years old," he said. "Can you believe it?"

"No," I said. "It doesn't seem possible."

Margaret smiled. "Such a sweet age."

I sipped my wine and glanced around the cozy kitchen, trying to wrap my mind around the passage of time. Eleven years with Sophia. Ten without my mother. So many birthdays and holidays and special occasions right here with Daniel and Margaret. Somehow they'd become my substitute family, the people I could count on in a pinch.

"So, Tracy," Margaret asked. "Have you decided about Thanksgiving?"

Her voice was casual, but she was watching me closely. She was a big Dr. Kinder fan, like all the other women I knew. She'd met him once and told me he was "quite a catch." She couldn't understand why I wouldn't want to join him for Turkey Day. Or marry him, for that matter.

"Well," I said. "I'd love to come here again, if that's okay with you."

"Of course," she assured me. "You're always welcome. That goes without saying."

"I can bake some pies. Maybe apple and pecan? Nobody ate the pumpkin last time."

"That would be wonderful," she said. "We all love your pies."

"Everything okay with you and the good doctor?" Daniel asked.

"Not really," I said. "I think we've reached the end of our road."

It was a relief to say it out loud, to make it official.

"Oh, Tracy." Margaret sounded heartbroken, as if someone had died. "I'm so sorry."

"It's okay," I told her. "It's better for both of us."

To Whom It May Concern:

My son James graduated from Green Meadow High School in 1969. He was a sweet boy with a sunny personality. He wasn't the best at schoolwork or sports, but he had a lot of good friends and loved to make people laugh. He always appreciated the food I cooked for him, especially my mashed potatoes and gravy. He could never get enough of that.

In 1970 my son James was drafted into the Army. He didn't want to go, but his father believed it was his duty and I agreed. That was how we were raised. James was obedient to our wishes and went to Vietnam to fight for his country. He died in November of 1971 and was buried with full military honors. I miss him terribly and grieve for all the life he did not get a chance to live.

These days very few people remember my son James, who died to keep us free, and that seems wrong to me. You should put him in your Hall of Fame so more people can learn about his sacrifice. That would give me great comfort in the final years of my life.

Sincerely,
Mrs. Marlene Haggerty (nee DeMarco)

ps—People knew him as Jimmy

* * *

Dear GMHS Hall of Fame Selection Committee:

Surely very few graduates of Green Meadow High School are more successful and distinguished than Matthew J. Keezer (GMHS class of 1973), President and CEO of the Keezer Auto Group, which has grown to encompass eight dealerships in two states. As Mr. Keezer likes to say, "We're not a group, we're an empire!"

Mr. Keezer isn't just an extraordinary business leader; he's also been a generous and tireless supporter of numerous local and national charities, along with his beautiful and talented wife, Jessica D'Alito Keezer (GMHS class of 1992). Mr. Keezer's motto has always been "Community First!"

Mr. Keezer has stated publicly many times that the foundation of his enormous success in life was built during his four years at GMHS: "High school was where I learned that with hard work and a positive attitude, truly anything is possible. I'm so grateful to my teachers and my fellow students for inspiring me to reach for the stars." It seems only fitting that GMHS would recognize Mr. Keezer's myriad achievements and contributions by welcoming him into your Hall of Fame. He certainly deserves the honor!

Thank you for your consideration.

> *Sincerely,*
> *Desiree Forest*
> *Director of Communications*
> *Keezer Auto Group*

PS—Biographical "sizzle reel" attached. Let me know if you need anything else!

*   *   *

Yo Mr. Weede!

I'm not sure if you remember me. Greg Filipek? Class of 2004? You suspended me once for making fart noises during a DARE assembly? Does that ring a bell? Three days seemed a little harsh at the time, but you were right. I should have listened to the DARE people. It would have saved me years of trouble.

So here's the thing. I heard about your Hall of Fame and I'd like to nominate myself. Can I do that? If not, I can probably find someone else to do it for me. Maybe my old buddy Mark Gaspar? He works for UPS now, in case you were wondering.

I know you're probably like there is no effing way that Greg Filipek belongs in anything except the D-bag Hall of Fame and I wouldn't blame you for thinking that, but only because you have no idea of the amazing feat I accomplished on February 8, 2006 when I was a student at the University of Scranton. (Full disclosure: I did not graduate from the University of Scranton, due to laziness and substance abuse issues that I'm currently dealing with. Also I cheated a lot in high school which as you once said was only cheating myself. True dat.)

Okay, back to the story. On February 8, 2006 I went to a sandwich shop known as Big Sal's and took the Big Sal's Challenge. The Big Sal's Challenge is a gigantic submarine sandwich that's as long as your arm and fatter too. I'm not lying it's HUGE. The rules of the Challenge are if you eat it by yourself in a half hour or less it's free. At the time I'm referring to only seven people had ever won the Big Sal's Challenge. Their pictures are up on the wall at Big Sal's.

Mr. Weede, I've made a lot of mistakes in my life. I've been in rehab three times. I let my parents down. I let my friends down. I let my ex-wife down, and a couple other women who made the not-great decision to get involved with me. I'm not a good father and have not always been as reliable about paying child support as I should have been.

But I ate that sandwich in twenty-two minutes! The whole friggin' thing. That's gotta be worth something. I swear if you don't believe me just go to Big Sal's in Scranton, Pennsylvania.

My picture's right there on the wall.

Your former student,
Greg F.

* * *

Dear Hall of Fame Selection Committee:

My beloved father, Walter Finley, graduated from Green Meadow High School in 1952. He attended Drew University and worked for many years as a CPA specializing in tax preparation for individuals and small businesses. He had an office on Center Street, right next to the bakery that has since become a Starbucks.

My father was also an author of some renown, publishing six novels under the pen name of W. K. Finn. His books are all out of print today, but they were well-received at the time of their publication, and one of them, Blue Meadow Fugue *(1973, Dark Horse Press), is widely considered to be a masterpiece. Professor Marcus Dowling of Fanning College called it "a late modernist gem from a writer who deserves a wider audience." The poet Grant Pasko praised* Blue Meadow Fugue *as "a tour-de-force of interiority . . . [a] painstaking and eerily beautiful reconstruction of the inner life of a twelve-year-old boy . . . [and] a vivid portrait of suburban America in the aftermath of a cataclysmic war." The critic Marcia Franck recently included* Blue Meadow Fugue *in her listicle, "20 Forgotten Novels Worth a Second Look."*

I have included a copy of Blue Meadow Fugue, *along with a SASE, for your perusal. I would appreciate it very much if you could return the book when you're done reading it. I have only eight copies left, and each one of them is precious to me. He was a true artist and a genuinely kind person and the best dad a little girl could have wished for. He died in 2015 after a long struggle with Parkinson's. I hope you will honor his memory as I do.*

Sincerely,
Phyllis Finley Wenderoth

- 11 -

Nate Cleary

We divided the most promising candidates among ourselves for further research. One of the names I got was Kelly Harbaugh, class of 2016, who'd dropped out of college and become a successful ASMR artist under the name of WhisperFriend47. That was how I happened to be watching a video called *You Look Soooo Pretty Tonight* while eating my Grape-Nuts on a Tuesday morning.

It was a simple concept, one girl pretending to do another girl's makeup, going through the whole routine, all the different brushes and pencils and creams, and offering a lot of compliments along the way.

"I wish I had your natural beauty," Kelly whispered. "You make it look so effortless."

All you could see were Kelly's face, her neck, and the top of her shoulders. Sometimes she held up her hands so you could see her perfectly manicured, sky-blue fingernails. She kept tapping those nails against hard surfaces—the makeup cases and bottles, the top of her desk, the screen of her laptop—and when she did this, she whispered the words *Tap Tap Tap* really fast (I guess some people get off on that). Mostly, though, she just focused on the makeup.

"I'm going to start with a hydrating primer," she said, holding up a neon-green tube. "This is the Flower Girl Coconut Water Exhilarator. *Tap Tap Tap.* It's what I always use when I want a fresh and shimmery look. I think you'll like it. *Tap Tap Tap.*"

Objectively speaking, the video was boring as shit, but I couldn't take my eyes off it. Kelly's lips were amazing—plump and pink and glossy—and she licked them a lot. If my father hadn't interrupted, I might have watched the whole thing in one sitting.

"Morning, champ." He patted me on the shoulder as he passed.

I shut the laptop and sat up straight. I'd been leaning pretty close to the screen.

"Morning."

"Little early for porn," he said.

"It's not porn," I told him, though I could feel myself blushing. "It's the Hall of Fame."

Lily Chu

There's a shelf in the back of the library that has all the GMHS year-books going back to 1949, the first year the school existed. The original yearbook was called *The Memory Bank*, and they kept that name until 1962, when for some reason it got changed to *Reflections*, the lame title we still use today.

During my free period, I opened the *Reflections* from 1969 and scanned the rows of senior portraits. I thought I'd find a bunch of Woodstock hippies, but the teenagers of Green Meadow didn't seem to know what year it was. The boys were mostly clean-cut in jackets and ties; a lot of the girls had hairdos that flipped up at the shoulders and collared dresses that buttoned at the neck. They were a very formal, very white crowd, only twenty or so Black students in the entire graduating class. It's still pretty white around here, but a little less so. Maybe forty Black people now, at least that many Asians, and a handful of Latinx people as well. Also, we get to submit our own photos, so our yearbooks feel a lot more colorful and visually diverse. And we all smile, which was totally not the case fifty years ago. They were pretty serious back then.

James Haggerty didn't look like a soldier. He was just a skinny kid with a bad complexion and an oversized Adam's apple. He seemed a little worried, almost like he knew something bad was coming. Beneath his photo, he'd listed a few special memories: *Camping with Ziggy and Slim. Junior Prom with Ellen. Summer weekends at Seaside. White Castle Emergency! More gravy, ma. Farewell, Green Meadow.*

I took out my phone and snapped a picture of his senior portrait, in case anyone on the Committee wanted to know what he looked like. For some reason, I kept staring at it throughout the day, the way you poke at a sore tooth with your tongue, even though you know it's going to hurt.

Nate Cleary

So the weird thing is, I actually knew Kelly Harbaugh. She was my counselor at summer camp back when I was in middle school, which was kind of a rough period in my life.

You wouldn't know it from looking at me now, but I used to be really short. Other kids (and a few asshole adults) used to call me Tiny Man and Little Natey, which for some reason didn't bother me for most of my childhood. It helped that I was really good at soccer, and always had a lot of friends.

I didn't get self-conscious about my size until sixth grade. Kids I'd known my whole life were suddenly sprouting up, leaving me in the dust. Bigger, less-talented players were pushing me around on the soccer field, using their weight to bump me off the ball. I didn't even bother to jump for headers anymore.

So I was pretty anxious when I got to the sleepaway camp that Green Meadow Youth Soccer sponsored every summer. I was twelve years old and I felt like everyone was staring at me, whispering about my bony rib cage and tiny hairless dick, and I guess Kelly noticed my discomfort, and took me under her wing.

I had really delicate features back then, and she used to tell me how good-looking I was. *You're gonna be such a heartthrob, Nate. I wish you were my age so you could be my boyfriend.* She touched me all the time, running her fingers through my hair, rubbing sunscreen onto my face and shoulders, letting me sit on her lap. We messed around a lot in the pool, swimming through each other's legs, seeing who could hold their breath underwater for longer. If there were chicken fights, we would always partner up. I would climb onto her shoulders, and she would wrap her hands around my ankles, and we would take on any challengers. And the whole time, my feet were brushing against her boobs, which were a little too big for her bikini top—it was blue with white stars, I remember that very clearly—and it made me excited in a way that she couldn't help but notice, because my crotch was pressed right up against the back of her neck.

Nate, she would say in this fake-shocked voice. *What's going on up there?*

Nothing, I would say, not very convincingly, which always made her laugh, and the motion of her shoulders just made everything worse.

No worries, she would tell me. *It's all good.*

It was just a one-week camp. She hugged me on the last day, pressed her lips against my ear, and whispered, *You're my favorite,* and I told her she was mine too, and that was it, the end of our summer fling.

Lily Chu

Clem and I liked to FaceTime late at night, after I was done with my homework. I had to whisper so I wouldn't wake my parents, but Clem was okay with that. They said it was hot when I whispered.

"Hey, Clem."

"Hey, Lils."

There was a little hump of silence, a shy moment when I didn't know what to say. It happened every time we talked, right at the beginning. It was like we'd never even met before, let alone had sex or said, *I love you*, or cried together for hours on the last day of Code Camp. All that seemed like a distant dream, a story I'd read over the summer and only vaguely remembered. But then it passed, the way it always did.

"I miss you," I said.

Clem was in their dorm room, sitting up in bed, wearing the gigantic gray sweatshirt they always slept in. They looked adorable, as usual, blond hair buzzed to a stubble and those lips that were so good to kiss, even when they were dry and chapped.

"Awww," Clem said. "I miss you too. How was your day?"

"Okay, I guess. But this Hall of Fame thing is so depressing. Just one boring white person after another."

"Still no POC?"

"Nope. No queer people, either. And hardly any women. It's kinda fucked up."

"So no one interesting?"

"There's this one kid who died in Vietnam. He didn't want to join the Army, but his parents made him."

"That sucks."

"I know, right? He looks so sad in his yearbook picture."

We were quiet for a while, and I couldn't help thinking about my own parents, who would never make me join the Army. They loved me so much, but they didn't really know me anymore. I didn't want it to be that way, but I didn't know how to change it.

"There's this other guy," I said. "He ate a really big sandwich."

Nate Cleary

I didn't speak to Kelly again until my first day at GMHS.

I was five foot five by then and I'd started shaving—the previous year had been one more or less constant and very awkward growth spurt—and she didn't even recognize me when I stopped her in the hall.

I'm Nate, I said. *Nate Cleary? You were my Junior Counselor at Soccer Camp?*

She studied me for a few seconds, and then she faked a smile. She was a senior that year, even prettier than I remembered.

Oh, hi there, she said in a bored voice, the way you'd speak to someone you barely knew, a person who meant nothing to you. *Welcome to high school.*

I saw her every day for the next nine months, and she never said hi to me, never smiled, never gave the slightest hint that she remembered our summer, all that time I'd spent sitting on her lap or perched on her shoulders, the fact that I was her favorite.

It bothered me for a while and then I got over it, or thought I did, because people change and life moves on, blah blah blah. And then she graduated, and I forgot all about her until I started watching those WhisperFriend videos.

Some part of me was impressed, for sure. It was pretty cool to see a person from my hometown, someone I actually *knew*, having so much success at such a young age. But I guess she must have hurt me more than I'd realized, because my main feeling was just like, *Fuck her.* I didn't care how many views she got on YouTube, or how much money she made, or how many people said they loved her in the comments; she'd treated me like shit for a whole year, and there was no way in hell I was voting her into the Hall of Fame.

- 12 -

Tracy Flick

I set the timer on my phone, lit a candle, and sat cross-legged on the floor. The house was quiet; the room was dim. I focused on the candle flame, the way it quivered and swayed, reacting to subtle changes in the air, and yet remaining resolute, true to its nature.

Be the flame, I told myself.

That wasn't my mantra. It was just a thought I was having, a way to collect myself and create a space for my intention.

The right side of my neck was itchy.

I scratched my neck.

Be the flame.

I started my meditation practice four years ago, after I was diagnosed with hypertension. It seemed unfair, because I wasn't even forty, and I was in really good shape. I'd stopped doing marathons, but I still ran at least three times a week, and did lots of planks and crunches on my off days (you should see my abs). My doctor wanted to write a prescription, but I hated the idea of starting down that path, losing control of my body, taking pills for the rest of my life. There had to be a better way.

I didn't love it at first. It went against my most basic inclination, which was to always be *doing something*. Sitting quietly with my breath felt lazy and self-indulgent, a form of weakness.

Very not me.

And yet, as difficult as it was, I could see the point right away. The loud voice in my head, the one I couldn't always control, would sometimes go quiet, and a different one would take over. A voice that was gentler and more forgiving, less angry and defensive. It was such a relief, and it made a big difference in my blood pressure. Twenty points on the systolic number, sometimes thirty.

Over time I started to figure out what worked for me and what didn't. I tried classes and retreats, but I could never relax with other people around. The same with the apps. The teacher's voice always felt like an intrusion, a violation of my solitude. The only place I could meditate was my own house; the only voice I could tolerate inside my head was my own.

I'll crush you, Tracy.

Be the flame.

I have a problem sometimes with obsessive thoughts—negative phrases that repeat on a loop during my sessions.

I'll crush you, Tracy.

You weren't supposed to resist these negative thoughts, or try to silence them. You were just supposed to observe them as they passed through your mind, let them drift away like smoke.

I'll crush you, Tracy.

For some reason, Kyle's ridiculous Ping-Pong taunt had gotten stuck in my head. I wasn't sure why; it was just harmless trash talk, and it was probably true, because I hadn't played Ping-Pong since middle school, and I wasn't even that great back then.

I'll crush you, Tracy.

Part of what irritated me was his condescending tone, the breezy assumption—without any evidence whatsoever—that I was an unworthy opponent and my defeat a foregone conclusion. Also, I hated that word: *crush*. The harshness of it, the utter finality, as if you'd been flattened beyond recognition, like a bug under someone's shoe.

You're a nobody.

That was another bad phrase orbiting my consciousness that fall.

No one knows your name.

I needed to pee.

I was sure of it.

But then I took a moment and remembered that I'd peed right before I lit my candle. I did that sometimes when my thoughts were making me uncomfortable. Distracted myself. Tried to escape.

Stay put, I told myself. *Focus on your breath.*

Be the flame.

I never wanted to be famous, not really. It was more that fame was the necessary precondition for, and inevitable by-product of, the thing I really did want, which was to be the first woman President of the United States.

I know, there's nothing more pathetic than a person talking about a dream that never happened, one that never even came close. It just makes you look like a fool. But being President wasn't some girlish fantasy of mine, some cute little idea that dissolved at the first contact with reality.

Being President was my ambition, not my dream.

There's a difference.

And it wasn't a crazy ambition. Whatever it is that a person needs to reach a goal like that, I had it in me, I knew I did. Even back in high school. Especially then. I was smart, I was tough, I had an incredible capacity for hard work, and I believed in myself. No imposter syndrome for me. And beyond that was my actual superpower, which was that I wanted it more than anyone else. Trust me, you didn't want to get in my way.

I could see the path laid out in front of me. I graduated Phi Beta Kappa from Georgetown, and worked as a congressional intern for one glorious summer. I remember how amazing that felt, flashing my ID, nodding to the security guard as I entered the Capitol Building in my navy-blue pantsuit, like I'd willed it to happen, like I'd granted my own deepest wish.

I went straight from undergrad to law school, also at Georgetown, because I knew what I wanted and where I needed to be.

I saw myself as a budding prosecutor. Those were years when being tough on crime was considered a virtue, and that suited me just fine. I liked rules and laws—I still do—and I believed that people who broke them should be punished to the fullest extent possible. Eventually a high-profile case would come my way, and I would go on TV and talk about order and justice and the righteous vengeance of the state, and people would remember my name. When the time was right, I would run for office. Congresswoman Flick. Senator Flick. Attorney General Flick. And who knows, maybe even . . .

Then I got the phone call.

My mother was everything to me. My fiercest advocate, my best friend, my entire family. The source of my dreams and my determination. She couldn't use them, so she passed them onto me. They were my inheritance.

It was hard for both of us when I left for college. Long distance was expensive back then, so we only talked on the phone once or twice a week. Mainly we communicated through the mail. She wrote me every single day. Long handwritten letters full of advice. Newspaper clippings about successful women. Old photos of the two of us. Brief affirmations scrawled on blank postcards.

You're the best!!!

Congrats on the Dean's List!!!

I'm the luckiest mother in the world!!!

The phone call that changed everything didn't come from her. It was from our downstairs neighbor and longtime landlord, Shirley Del Vecchio.

Tracy, honey. I'm sorry to bother you. I know how busy you are.

No worries, I said, though I was already worried, because Shirley had never called me at school before. *Is everything okay?*

No, honey. Things are not okay. They haven't been okay for a while now.

My mom was sick. It turned out she'd been diagnosed with MS during my sophomore year in college, but I didn't know that, because she hadn't told me. She'd meant to, she later explained, but it was always the wrong time to break the news—I had midterms, I had finals, I had that long research paper on Adam Smith. I had that obnoxious neighbor who kept me awake at night. I didn't need any more stress in my life.

What's harder to understand is my own blindness. Didn't I see that she was weak and feverish, having trouble reading and getting around? I did and I didn't. Sometimes when I was home, she seemed fine, her old self. And if she was having an attack, all she ever said was that she wasn't feeling well.

It's no fun getting old, honey.

The truth is, I didn't get home that much or stay very long when I did. You could blame me for being self-absorbed—I certainly blamed myself—but that was the deal my mother and I had struck a long time ago, probably on the day I was born. I was the one with the mission; she was just support staff. That was the way *she* wanted it, and that was the way we lived.

The deception only worked as long as it did because her symptoms were mild at first, and her remissions lasted for months. The Del Vecchios helped a lot too. Shirley drove my mom to the doctor's when she couldn't get there on her own, and she nursed my mother on days when she couldn't get out of bed. And she never said a word to me.

That spring, though, their conspiracy collapsed. Shirley's daughter, who lived in Virginia, gave birth to twins. Shirley and her husband, Joe, wanted to go there for a couple of weeks, meet the new babies, and pitch in with child care, but they were worried about leaving my mother alone in the house.

She's not in great shape, Shirley told me. *The stairs are hard for her. Everything's hard. She needs a lot of help.*

I remember standing there, my mind going quiet, the way it does sometimes when you get bad news you don't want—can't bring yourself—to believe.

Honey, she said. *Are you there?*

I put a few things in my backpack and got on the train. I didn't know that I was leaving law school forever. I thought I was going home for a few days, a few weeks at the most. But she was so much sicker than I'd imagined. I ended up taking my final exams from home—I aced them, for what it's worth—and canceled my summer internship, which was a huge disappointment. Then I took a leave of absence for the fall semester, and another for the spring.

At the time, these seemed like temporary setbacks—*until she got back on her feet*—because neither of us could have accepted the possibility that our new arrangement might be permanent. Two years went by before I was able to admit to myself that I was no longer on leave from Georgetown. I was just living at home, taking care of my mom.

Those years are a blur in my memory, but not a bad one, not completely. We watched a lot of old movies and played way too much Scrabble. We sat in waiting rooms, nodding politely to the other sick people, many of whom told us we looked like sisters, which always made my mom very happy. I learned to cook and clean, which I hadn't been allowed to do in the past because she hadn't wanted me wasting my valuable time. I took up long-distance running, leaving the house at the crack of dawn, regardless of the weather, pushing myself past the pain into a state that on good days was something close to bliss, or at least as close as I ever got. I became very familiar with my mother's body. For a while, this embarrassed both of us, and then we got over it. It was a comfort to me, being a comfort to her.

The Del Vecchios were so generous. They actually paid out of their own pocket to install a stairlift, and they let us build a ramp for her wheelchair. They're gone now—they moved to Florida—but that ramp is still there, and I still think of their kindness every time I drive past our old house.

My mom retired on full disability, but the benefits only covered a portion of her salary, so I worked when I could to help keep us afloat. I spent my first summer at home as a market research associate, which is a nice way of saying that I harassed people at the mall for minimum wage, stepping into their path and saying, *Hi there, can I ask you a few questions about athlete's foot?* It was horrible work, full of frosty brush-offs and rude comments, made even worse by the fact that I sometimes accidentally accosted former classmates, who couldn't understand why the person they'd voted Most Likely to Succeed was standing in front of them with a clipboard and a frozen smile, demanding to know their opinion about sugarless gum.

After that I signed on with a temp agency. I spent my days filing invoices, sorting shipping manifests into color-coded piles, making copies of annual reports. One week the agency sent me to an insurance company in the World Trade Center—the only time I ever set foot in those doomed towers—where I typed rejection letters to heartbroken people, explaining that the cause of their loved one's death—lightning strike, small plane crash, hunting accident, suicide, avalanche, every sort of random tragedy—was not covered by their life insurance policy, which meant that no payment was forthcoming, and no appeal was possible.

Substitute teaching felt like a big step up from that. The pay was okay, the hours were decent, the schedule was flexible. More important, it seemed professional in a way that temping hadn't, and more personal too, like I could be my true self again, and not just an anonymous cog in a commercial transaction. School had always been my chosen arena, the place where I shined the brightest. I still remember my first day on the job, standing in front of an Algebra 2 class in Grover Township, writing *Tracy Flick* on the board like an autograph. It felt like a homecoming, like my exile was over.

You failed.

That one blinked in my mind like a neon sign.

You failed.

It was irrefutable. I wasn't a Congresswoman. I wasn't a Senator. I wasn't the President. I wasn't even the Principal of Green Meadow High School. But I also understood that failure wasn't the whole story.

You did the best you could.

I was a dedicated, hardworking sub, and they liked me at Grover. I got certified and taught there for eleven years. I advised the Student Government, supervised Mock Trial, and helped create a Model UN program that's still going strong. All that time, I was caring for my mother, and attending graduate school on nights and weekends. I had a child, earned my PhD in Education Administration, and took the job I have now. That's not nothing.

I'm not ashamed of the life I've made for myself. Or at least that's what I thought, until this Hall of Fame thing started up. It saddened me in a way I hadn't anticipated. I kept imagining what would happen if my old high school started a Hall of Fame and my name came up for consideration. What would people say? *She's an Assistant Principal. She helped her mom when she got sick.* That wasn't gonna cut it. Nope. Not good enough. No Hall of Fame for you, Tracy Flick.

You're a nobody.

*　*　*

After thirty minutes, the timer went off and I blew out the candle. I had a few things to do before bed, but I wasn't ready to move yet, so I just sat there for a while, breathing quietly in the darkness.

You failed.

You did the best you could.

You failed.

You did the best you could.

Both those statements were true, and I accepted the mixed verdict. I was an adult; I had no choice. But I desperately wanted to go back in time, to find the girl I used to be and tell her how sorry I was for letting her down, that fierce young woman who never had a chance, the one who got crushed.

13

Vito sat up and rubbed his eyes. He had no idea what time it was. *Breaking Bad* was on TV with the sound off, the end of season 2 or the beginning of season 3, he wasn't sure which.

The place was a mess. Clothes on the floor, a pizza box flopped open on the coffee table—two sweaty slices remaining—next to a tipped-over container of ibuprofen and a partially disassembled handgun.

It was creepy to see the pistol—it was a good one, a Sig Sauer P320, a Christmas gift from his soon-to-be-ex-brother-in-law— sitting right out in the open like that. All he'd meant to do was clean it, because it had been years since he'd fired the thing, and the maintenance was long overdue. Only problem was, he couldn't remember how to take it apart. He'd sat through a tedious instructional video on YouTube, but the process turned out to be more complicated than he remembered, and in the end, he just said fuck it and took a nap.

I'm unwell, he reminded himself, and for some reason, the word made him feel a little better.

Unwell.

Not sick, exactly, though that was what he'd been telling the school for the past three days—bad flu, maybe strep—and he'd given the same excuse to Wesley, who'd been texting repeatedly, trying to figure out why Vito had skipped the last two meetings.

Have you been drinking?

Jesus Christ, Wesley. Give me a little credit.

But the sad truth was, he *had* been drinking. Just once, a few days ago, on the Sunday after Thanksgiving, and it wasn't even because he was that desperate for booze. It had just been a really shitty day, the capstone of a really shitty long holiday weekend. Susie wouldn't even let him stop by for a piece of pie and a fucking turkey sandwich with his kids, supposedly because they didn't "feel safe" with their own father, which was a crock of shit, because he would never do anything to hurt them, and she knew that just as well as he did.

He put on his coat, walked down to the Last Call, and drank himself into oblivion along with three old-timers in their usual spots at the bar. They all nodded politely when he sat down, as if they remembered him well and weren't the least bit surprised to see him.

It was harder than he expected to put the gun in his mouth. There wasn't any danger—he'd removed the magazine—but it was just one of those things your body rebelled against, like standing on the edge of a cliff and looking down.

His idea was to take a selfie and email it to Susie, along with a humorous caption.

Season's Greetings.
Thinking of you.
I'm a little unwell.
Is this what you want?

The first picture was a disappointment. The lighting was too stark and his hair was a mess, but mostly it was just the expression on his face. His brow was deeply furrowed, and his eyes looked glassy and a little desperate, like maybe he wasn't fooling around.

He scooted away from the lamp, fixed his hair, and wrapped his lips around the barrel. Like a lot of things in life, it was easier the second time. He raised his left arm and gazed up at the screen with a cool, defiant expression. He was just about to snap the photo when the phone vibrated in his hand, shocking the hell out of him. He took the gun out of his mouth and checked the caller ID.

GMHS, it said. *Green Meadow, NJ.*

14

Dear Committee:

I'm sorry if I missed the nomination deadline, but I hope it's not too late to put in a good word for Reggie Morrison, who was one of the superstars of Green Meadow football during the glory years of the early 1990s, when Larry Holleran was Coach and Vito Falcone was quarterback.

Yes, everyone remembers Vito, but what about the other member of the so-called "Dynamic Duo?" Unlike Vito, Reggie didn't make it into the NFL, but that was just bad luck. Bad luck and racism. Nobody likes to hear that about their hometown but it's true. And I'm just gonna say it flat out— Reggie was the better athlete and the better person. He made Vito look good, not the other way around.

I know—Reggie did something wrong and everyone wants to erase him from history. But there are two sides to every story— more than two sides—and Reggie deserves better from Green Meadow. If there was any justice, you would put him in the Hall of Fame.

Sincerely,
A Concerned Alum

- 15 -

Jack Weede

Once a week or so, when I woke up before dawn and couldn't get back to sleep, I slipped out of bed and took the motor home for a spin. You couldn't just leave it sitting in the driveway, the battery draining away, the tires flattening themselves against the blacktop. As the salesman told me right before I drove it off the lot, the Winnebago needed exercise, just like a person did.

I also needed the practice. The RV was only a little smaller than a school bus, and it took skill and courage to navigate it through the world. The biggest problem was making a right turn, so simple in a car. You had to swing your front end way out into oncoming traffic, and then immediately swerve back into your own lane, spinning the wheel like a maniac to straighten out. Pulling away from a curb was similarly challenging, as I'd learned on one of my early outings, when I oversteered and clipped a parking meter on Fuller Street, leaving a small but nasty gash in the metal above my right rear tire. I was upset about the damage, but Alice shrugged it off.

It was bound to happen sometime. Now you don't have to worry about it.

She wanted to join me on my practice runs, but I never had the heart to roust her out of bed at five thirty in the morning. She'd been sleeping so deeply the past few months, as if she were repaying a debt to her body. Sometimes I just stood there and watched her breathe, thinking about the fragility of our lives, and how easily things could have been otherwise.

The streets were pretty empty at that time of the morning, no one awake except for a few dog walkers and the guy who delivered the *Ledger*, rolling by in his old Mazda and flinging newspapers onto the dead lawns, some of which were decorated with blinking reindeer and huge inflatable snowmen. I felt like the king of that sleepy world, perched high in my captain's chair, driving my mobile home past all the stationary ones, like a dream where everyone was frozen in place but me.

I always took the same route on these morning drives, winding down through the hills of Poplar Ridge into the flats of Green Meadow. I drove past the high school and felt a pang in my chest as I rumbled by, a swell of premature nostalgia for the institution I'd led for so many years and would soon be leaving. It looked uncharacteristically serene in the light of dawn, a flat-roofed, two-story, pink-and-brown structure, reflected like the Taj Mahal on the surface of the small oval pond that separated the building from the road, and somehow rescued it from pure utilitarian ugliness. We needed a new high school, I understood that better than anyone, but I'd be sorry to see the old one go. So much of my life, so many of my best memories, were contained within those unassuming walls.

Beyond the soccer field, I turned onto Henley Boulevard and cruised through the residential neighborhood affectionately known as "The Ladies"—street after street with names like Carla Drive and Heather Court and Roberta Road. Kyle Dorfman's mansion was on MaryBeth Way, and I couldn't help slowing down and gawking like a tourist as I passed.

The house was ridiculous—three misaligned boxes stacked one on top of the other, like a section of an unsolved Rubik's Cube—but it exerted a strange magnetism. The top story was perched so precariously on the middle one that it seemed as if a strong wind might knock it over. At the same time, the stainless steel exterior gave off an otherworldly, faintly radioactive glow, making the rest of the houses on the street look even more dull and hopeless than they already were. I couldn't understand why Kyle would want to live like that, glorifying himself at the expense of his neighbors. He must have suffered a terrible narcissistic injury as a child; there was a hole inside of him that could never be filled, no matter how much money and adulation he shoveled in.

I felt sorry for him, I really did.

At the bottom of Henley, I turned right onto Thurman Avenue, the stretch with Home Depot and Target and the Wagon Wheel Diner, which was actually a Thai place now, though they'd kept the old name and the sign for some reason. Everyone said it was great, though I wasn't much of a Thai guy myself. A quarter of a mile beyond the Wagon Wheel was Lost Meadow Village, a sprawling garden apartment complex at the edge of town, and another important landmark on my personal map.

Diane Blankenship lived in Unit 17, Apartment C. Whenever I drove by, I felt a powerful, almost dreamlike urge to ring her doorbell, as if it might be possible to travel back in time and pick up where we'd left off so abruptly, Diane greeting me at the door in a translucent slip, pulling me inside, her mouth on mine, her fingers already working on my belt.

I only went there four or five times, and even that was too many, because we were both well-known figures in town, and there was nothing private or secluded about Lost Meadow Village. I always took the trouble to disguise myself, but my disguise was pathetic, just a floppy Australian bush hat and a pair of blue-tinted aviator sunglasses. And I drove there in my own car, the same silver Lexus I parked every weekday in the space that said RESERVED FOR MR. WEEDE.

Of course I got recognized. On my final visit, two sophomores—Alma Chung and Elena Brenner—walked out of Unit 17 just as I was heading up the front path. The girls froze in their tracks.

Mr. Weede? Alma said. *What are you doing here?*

It was a very good question.

I, uh . . . I'm visiting my aunt . . . Muriel. I haven't seen her in quite a while. She lives in Unit . . . 18, I believe. I think that's the number.

I was always a good liar when I needed to be.

This is 17, Elena said. *18's over there.*

So it is. I shook my head, amused by my own incompetence.

My grandmother lives in 17, Alma informed me. *Maybe she knows your aunt.*

I doubt it, I said. *Muriel's kind of a shut-in.*

You know who else lives here? Elena declared. *Front Desk Diane.*

Is that so? I said, and then caught myself. *I mean, I know she lives around here, I just didn't know which . . .*

She's a nice person, Alma observed. *She always checks on my grandmother.*

She's very nice, I agreed. *Well, it's a pleasure to see you girls. I should, uh . . . my aunt's waiting . . .*

They nodded, and headed on their way. I started in the direction of Unit 18, in case they were watching, which of course they were, because kids are always watching. Elena called out, *Nice hat, Mr. Weede!* and I gave them a friendly wave without turning around.

I don't know what I was thinking in those days, how I imagined I'd get away with it.

I guess I wasn't thinking at all.

Or maybe I wanted to get caught.

To burn it all down.

The only way I can explain it is to say that I was a little crazy back then, a little desperate. I was in my late fifties, bored with my marriage and frustrated with my job. Yes, I was Principal, but that was the last stop on the train. There was nowhere to go after that except out to pasture.

It wasn't enough. Not even close.

Also, I was getting old. I could feel the early warnings. Little aches and mysterious tingles. Afternoon catnaps at my desk. Trouble putting my socks on. On top of that, my dick had begun letting me down, which was the greatest betrayal of all. Alice told me it didn't matter to her, and I knew she was telling the truth. But it mattered to me.

It mattered a lot—more than I'd like to admit—so I spoke to my doctor, and at least that problem got fixed. I don't know what men did back before the medication. Did they just give up, say goodbye to all that? Because that really wasn't an option for me.

I was restless, looking for an adventure, a way to prove to myself that the story wasn't over. And Diane was right there in front of me— not young, but a lot younger than I was, and pretty, and emotionally adrift. No kids, abandoned by her jerk of an ex-husband. I could feel the dark energy pouring out of her, a familiar desperation. We teamed up like Bonnie and Clyde, and went on our little crime spree.

At least we didn't kill anyone.

Happy people don't do what we did. They don't fuck in the Principal's office in the middle of the day, with a bunch of co-workers on the other side of the door. They don't sneak off to the parking lot during halftime. She threw pebbles at my window one night at two in the morning, and I snuck downstairs and let her into the garage. She knelt down on the cold cement floor and gave me the best blowjob of my life, my wife asleep in our bed, my daughter home from college.

I don't know what would've happened if Alice hadn't gotten sick. There's a very good chance that Diane and I would've been caught; I could've lost my job, lost my family, ended my career in shame. Maybe Diane and I would've tried to make a go of it, to be a real couple in the real world instead of a pair of outlaws. Who knows. Maybe it would've worked.

It's all moot. You can't have an affair while your wife—the mother of your children—is dying. I mean, some guys can—Newt Gingrich did, if I remember correctly—but not me. And anyway, there was no point anymore. I had all the drama and adventure anyone needed, right in my own house. The real thing, life and death, sickness and health. Fucking your secretary is nothing compared to that.

Diane understood. She was a grown-up and a good person. The only thing that surprised me was that she stuck around at the main office. I thought she might give her notice, because it was awkward and painful for both of us, having to work together after everything we'd been through, to turn off those other feelings. I knew it was unfair, my assumption that she was the one who should leave, but it made sense: there were tons of jobs for secretaries and administrative assistants out there, many of which paid a lot more than she was making at the high school, and very few openings for Principals, especially for a man my age. But she was stubborn; she stayed right where she was—Front Desk Diane to the bitter end—and all the life went out of her. That was my fault, at least partly—I couldn't deny it—but there was nothing I could do to make it better, except leave her alone as much as possible.

Well, she'd finally outlasted me. In a few months, I'd be gone, and she'd be working for Tracy Flick, and I hoped that would be a comfort to her.

Right after Lost Meadow Village, I got on the Parkway and headed north to complete my journey. It was a humbling experience, merging the RV onto the highway, stomping on the gas pedal, waiting for a power surge that never arrived as everyone else zoomed past like I was standing still. It felt like the perfect metaphor for getting old and falling by the wayside.

I took the Grover exit and headed through the quaint downtown, feeling a familiar urgency in the region of my bladder. It was often like that, a race to get home and rush into the bathroom, one more indignity of advancing age. Of course, I could've stopped and availed myself of the pristine toilet on the RV, but I hated the idea of sully-ing it for the first time when I was only a few minutes from home.

I'd just passed the movie theater when an unmarked police car appeared in my rearview with exquisitely bad timing and flashed its lights. Despite my rising sense of alarm, I was able to pull over with-out too much trouble, though I did scrape my right front hubcap against the curb.

The cop was in plain clothes, a short, squat guy who moved with an unhurried swagger, leading with a belly other men might have tried to conceal. When I asked what I'd done wrong, he removed his sunglasses and grinned.

"Morning, Mr. Weede."

Oh God, I thought.

When you're the Principal, all the kids know you, but you can't possibly know all of them. And even if you did know them back in the day, you might not recognize them now. Fifteen or twenty years is a better disguise than a floppy hat.

"Help me out," I said. "I'm bad with names."

"Glenn Keeler. Class of '97."

"Oh wow," I said, though the name meant nothing to me. "Glenn Keeler. How about that? It's been quite a while."

"Sure has," he said. "I hear you're getting ready to retire."

"Yeah, I'm gonna miss it."

"Good to be the king, right?"

"Sometimes. When the crown's not too heavy."

He nodded, a little vaguely, and rubbed his stomach in a leisurely circular motion, as if he'd just had a very good meal. I held up my wallet.

"Do you, uh . . . need to see my license and registration?"

"Nah." He waved me off, a little sheepishly. "Just wanted to say hi. It's not every day you get to pull over your old Principal, right?"

"I guess not." I chuckled, not very convincingly. "If you don't mind, though, I really have to get going. I'm a running a little late this morning."

"Oh, sure," he said. "No worries. I didn't mean to—"

"It's okay." I started the engine, trying not to think about the pressure building inside of me, threatening to burst. "It was nice to—"

"Just one quick question," he said. "Are you really gonna put Vito Falcone in the Hall of Fame?"

"We haven't decided yet. There's a meeting next week."

"But it's gotta be Vito, right?" He gave me a searching look. "I mean, who else could it be?"

It was none of his business, but I really didn't have time for a big discussion.

"Just between us," I said. "I think Vito's got a very good chance."

"And he's coming to the ceremony?"

"I hope so." I shifted into gear and let up on the brake. "Wouldn't be much of an event if he didn't."

"That's what I figured," Glenn said, and then he muttered something else, but I wasn't listening anymore. I was too busy inching the RV away from the curb, a delicate maneuver that took all the skill and concentration I could muster in the best of times, and this was not the best of times.

- 16 -

Tracy Flick

The holidays were hard for me. I went through the motions for my daughter's sake—we trimmed the tree, we watched Charlie Brown and the Grinch, we went caroling with the neighbors—but we both knew that her real Christmas was with Daniel and Margaret and their extended family (two of their three adult children were married, and there were a couple of grandkids, which technically meant that she was "Aunt Sophia," though no one ever called her that). We'd tried alternating years for a while, but it was sad for her when she got stuck with me and had to miss out on all the fun at her father's house, three generations under one roof, not to mention Boomer. At her request, we switched to our current system, in which she joined me on Christmas Eve—that was when we opened our presents—and then I dropped her off at Daniel's, so she could be where the action was in the morning.

I didn't blame her. I was always a little mopey in December, missing my mom, who'd loved the holidays, and always made them feel special, even though it was just the two of us. I wished I could do the same thing for my own child—engulf her with love, make her believe she was enough for me, that we were enough for each other—but I didn't have it in me, and there was no use pretending. All I could do was hunker down and wait for January, which always felt like a fresh start, a chance to do better.

* * *

I wasn't in the mood for Kyle's Christmas party, but he reminded me that the entire School Board would be there, and that it would be a great opportunity for me to do some networking. So I put on the green velvet dress I'd inherited from my mother—we were exactly the same size—and drove over to his house.

I especially dislike arriving at parties, those awkward early moments when you have to wander through the crowd, searching for a familiar face. But I was spared that ordeal at the Dorfmans'. I barely had time to unbutton my coat before Kyle materialized with a big smile on his face.

"Dr. Flick!" He was wearing jeans and a thin, expensive-looking sweater that highlighted his improbable torso. "Welcome to my humble abode."

He said this with the appropriate level of irony. The ground floor was spectacular, a vast open space featuring a variety of living and dining areas—some sunken, some elevated—with an airy kitchen at one end, and an enormous stone fireplace at the other. The south-facing wall was floor-to-ceiling glass. The morning light must have been breathtaking.

"Come on," he said. "They're all waiting for you."

He led me through the party. Andrea Palladino, Charisse Turner, and Kitty Valvanos—the three women members of the School Board, a majority unto themselves—were gathered near the fireplace, drinking fancy cocktails and laughing like old friends.

"Look who's here," Kyle told them. "Our favorite Assistant Principal."

I didn't know these women personally—I'd only ever encountered them at official functions—but they greeted me warmly and welcomed me into their circle, insisting that I switch from champagne to a Pink Negroni, which was apparently the drink of the evening. It was small talk at first—holiday plans, the greatness of *Hamilton* (which I still hadn't seen), the new Indian restaurant downtown—

but we drifted, inevitably, to the subject of our kids, which led to a discussion of homework loads and standardized testing and accommodations for students with disabilities (Andrea's daughter had cerebral palsy and required a full-time classroom aide). They treated me like an expert, listening carefully to my opinions and recommendations, and I knew I'd made the right decision, getting myself out of the house and into the world.

At one point, Andrea and Kitty headed off to the bar, and I found myself alone with Charisse. Her son, Marcus, was a freshman at the high school, a three-sport athlete so talented that people had begun to compare him to Vito Falcone. Charisse herself was a partner at a big law firm in Newark.

"I know you're super busy," I told her. "But if you ever have a spare hour to meet with our Mock Trial team, the kids would be thrilled. It would be so inspiring for them to talk to a real-life litigator. And I'd love to hear your thoughts myself."

Her smile was equal parts pleasure and dismay.

"I'd like to," she said. "But I'm a little swamped right now."

"No pressure. It's an open invitation."

She gave me a quizzical look, as if she'd just remembered something.

"Didn't you go to law school?"

"Georgetown," I said. "But I never finished. There was a family emergency, and I had to come home. It's my road not taken."

There must have been a wistful note in my voice, because Charisse tried to cheer me up.

"You know, Tracy, it's never too late. You can always go back. We just hired an associate in his early fifties. He's a good lawyer."

Over the years, I'd occasionally fantasized about returning to law school—picking up that abandoned thread—but it was just that: a fantasy, a way to relieve whatever professional frustration I was feeling at the moment.

"Oh no," I assured her. "I'm right where I want to be. It's such a privilege working with high school students. All that potential. It's a gift."

"I'm glad to hear it." She touched her glass to mine. "We need people like you in our administration."

She finished her cocktail and set her empty glass on the mantelpiece. When she turned around, there was a sly look on her face, like we were done with the bullshit.

"I just have one question. What are we gonna do about our football coach? The man is an embarrassment. Seven losing seasons in a row? We need to find the next Coach Holleran. Someone who can get us back on the right track."

"I agree," I said, though I was sick of hearing people talk about Larry Holleran. "One hundred percent. It's time for a change."

While we were talking the room had been filling up, the noise level rising. Just as Andrea and Kitty returned, the lights dimmed and the Jackson Five's "ABC" exploded from hidden speakers: *A Boop Boop Buh Boo! A Boop Boop Boop Buh Boo!* Charisse asked if I wanted to dance, but I waved her off and made a hasty exit, moving against the tide of bodies surging onto the dance floor. I was almost out of the fray when I literally bumped into my ex-boyfriend, Philip, who was grinning goofily, spinning his fists like one of the Temptations. He stopped smiling and dropped his hands to his sides.

"Tracy," he said, with unpleasant surprise, and that was when I noticed the woman standing at his side. She was dark-haired and slender, with wary eyes and a face that looked ten years older than her body.

"Wow," I told him. "That was quick."

He shrugged, like I had no right to complain, and I really didn't. I was the one who'd broken up with him, the one who wouldn't even return his phone calls.

"Nice to see you," he said. "Happy holidays."

I meant to leave, but I stopped by the wall and turned around. I'd never seen Philip dance before, and my curiosity got the best of me.

He was okay, I suppose. He was definitely enjoying himself, pumping his arms and swinging his hips with determined middle-aged vigor. His companion was more relaxed, barely moving at all, except for her weirdly restless hands, which never stopped sculpting the air in front of her face.

I wasn't jealous, not really. I didn't love Philip, and I didn't want him back. But I couldn't help remembering how fortunate and hopeful I'd felt at the beginning of our relationship, the surprise of meeting a man who checked all the boxes and genuinely seemed to like me. All I'd had to do was let go a little, welcome him into my life, make the compromises everyone else made, but I couldn't manage it. I'd never been able to do that, to really open myself up to another person.

It's okay, I told myself. *You're on your own. That's just the way it is.*

I'm not sure how long I stood there. Two songs, maybe three. All I know for sure is that "1999" was playing when Marissa Dorfman appeared at my side. I hadn't seen her since the football game.

"Not in a dancing mood?" she asked.

"Maybe later," I lied.

She touched a finger to my sleeve, just above the elbow.

"I like your dress."

"Thanks. It was my mother's."

She didn't reply, but I could feel the question she wasn't asking.

"I miss her," I said.

She gave my arm a quick, supportive squeeze, and turned her gaze back to the dancers, all those flailing arms and happy faces. She was wearing a black dress, very simple, and her hair was gathered into a messy updo that was casual and glamorous at the same time.

"That's my ex," I said, nodding towards Philip. "We broke up at Thanksgiving."

"Really?" She gave me that startled look I'd received so many times before. "Dr. Kinder?"

"Yeah," I said. "Lucky me, right?"

She snorted and bumped me with her shoulder.

"Someone got lucky," she said. "But I don't think it was you."

117

- 17 -

Kyle Dorfman

We had the second Committee meeting in Jack's office. I would have preferred a leisurely meal at a good restaurant, but everybody else wanted to meet on school grounds. More time efficient for the administrators, and less disruptive for the students. Whatever. The majority rules.

It was a week before Christmas, and you could feel it inside the building—that giddy sense of winding down, slacking off, vacation right around the corner. A fair number of kids had decorated their lockers with wreaths and stockings, and a handful of proud nerds were walking around with fuzzy antlers on their heads. If I'd been their age, I might have been one of them.

I stopped by Tracy's office on the way in. She was hard at work, as usual, hammering away at her keyboard like she was mad at the letters.

"Knock, knock," I said from the doorway.

"Oh." She stopped typing and forced a smile. "Is it that time already?"

"I'm a little early." I walked over to the desk and handed her an envelope. "Just wanted to give you this. It's from Marissa."

Tracy studied the envelope with a puzzled expression. It was made of handcrafted pulp stock—turquoise flecked with lavender—and tied with a piece of twine.

"She took a paper-making class," I explained.

"Oh." Tracy looked surprised. "That's very . . . impressive."

"She's a big knitter too," I said. "If you need a winter hat, just say the word."

Tracy Flick

Front Desk Diane handed out the short list, then checked with Jack.

"Anything else?" she asked.

Diane was wearing a red sweater with a big white snowflake on the front, but her face looked drawn and anxious, devoid of holiday spirit. She'd been having a rough semester. A couple of weeks earlier, I'd found her crying in the Faculty and Staff Ladies' Room. When I asked what was wrong, she said it was nothing, just hormones, and I left it at that. We'd worked together for a long time, but I was her boss, not her friend.

"Thank you, Diane." Jack gave her a curt nod of dismissal. "I think we're all set."

She left the room, shutting the door softly behind her. Jack clapped his hands, calling the meeting to order.

"Okay, then. Here we are." He nodded slowly, acknowledging the solemn duty that was resting on our shoulders. "As you can see, we have a diverse array of candidates to consider, alumni with significant achievements in a wide variety of endeavors. Some young, some old, some living, some . . . no longer with us, I'm sorry to say." He observed a brief moment of silence, then brightened again. "I think our biggest challenge will be finding a common denominator, a standard of measurement that will allow us to compare apples and oranges without doing a disservice to either fruit."

He went on like that for a while—Jack had a weakness for lengthy preambles—but I was only half listening. I was still a bit perplexed by the envelope in my blazer pocket, the sweet, very brief note from Marissa—*Great to see you at the party! I really enjoyed our talk . . .*

121

xoxo, M.—followed by her cell number and email address, along with the postscript *Let's hang out soon!*

It seemed a little excessive. We'd only chatted for a few minutes, and then she'd gotten summoned by the caterer, and I'd slipped away without saying goodbye. It was a perfectly pleasant interaction, but it hardly warranted a handwritten note on handmade paper.

Lily Chu

The short list read as follows:

1. Vito Falcone, 1994 (Professional Athlete)
2. William Finley, aka W. K. Finn, 1952 (Accountant/Novelist)
3. James Haggerty, 1969 (Gold Star Veteran, Vietnam)
4. Kelly Harbaugh, aka WhisperFriend47, 2016 (Internet Personality)
5. Matthew J. Keezer, 1973 (Automobile Dealer)

Principal Weede had called it "a diverse array of candidates," and I guess there was some truth to that. The finalists came from different eras, they did different things, and yes, some of them were dead. There was even one woman in the group, which was definitely better than nothing, even if she was a college dropout who made videos with titles like *I Love Your Hair* and *Let's Make You Even Hotter*.

But come on. It was 2018—almost 2019—and five white people was the best we could do?

It was embarrassing.

Nate Cleary

We did the easy part first. Principal Weede said that his secretary had spoken to Vito Falcone, and that Vito had promised to attend the Induction Ceremony if he was selected for the Hall of Fame.

"In light of this excellent news," he said, "I propose a vote on the candidacy of Mr. Falcone. All in favor?"

He raised his hand, and Kyle and I did the same. After a brief hesitation, Dr. Flick joined the majority, followed a moment later by Lily, though she didn't look too happy about it.

"All righty." Principal Weede nodded his approval. "The Committee is unanimous. One down, one to go. Our next candidate is William Finley, the author. Did anyone else have a chance to look at his book?"

Kyle and I shook our heads. Dr. Flick said she'd skimmed it, but hadn't been too impressed. Lily said she'd stopped after the first chapter.

"It was too confusing. It just kept skipping around. I didn't know whose head I was in."

"That's a common modernist technique," Principal Weede explained. "I'm not sure it's aged very well. I guess that's an ixnay on Mr. Finley."

We bogged down after that. Everyone felt bad for James Haggerty, but not bad enough to put him in the Hall of Fame. Kelly Harbaugh did a little better. Weede and Kyle thought she'd be a refreshing choice, but Lily and Flick disagreed, on the grounds that it would send the wrong message to the girls of Green Meadow, what with Kelly being so focused on makeup and talking in that weird whispery voice. It came down to me—and like I said, fuck her—so she didn't get a majority, either.

"That leaves us with *Keezer*." Principal Weede made a sour face. "Personally, I'm not crazy about the idea of honoring a car salesman."

Nobody else was, either, so we just sat there and stared at one another.

Lily Chu

I didn't want to be a pain in the ass, especially so close to the holidays, but I didn't want to be a coward, either, so I forced my hand into the air.

"Yes, Lily?" Principal Weede gave me a sweet smile. "What's on your mind?"

"I was wondering about Reggie Morrison."

His smile disappeared. "What about him?"

"Um, I know the nomination came in late, but I did some research, and it's true—all the articles say he was just as good as Vito Falcone. They were both All-State and they both got big college scholarships. And Reggie scored more touchdowns. He still holds the school record. So it seems like it's only fair—"

"Reggie never made it to the NFL," Nate pointed out.

"I know," I said. "But when they were here—"

"Reggie's a little . . . controversial," Principal Weede told me. "I don't know if you know this, but he assaulted a police officer."

"The cop was off duty," I said. "And the charges were dropped, right?"

"It was a big mess, Lily." Principal Weede checked with Mr. Dorfman. "I really don't think we want to revisit all that, do we?"

"Not this year," Mr. Dorfman agreed. "I think we should probably stick to our list."

I glanced at Dr. Flick, hoping for a little support, but she wouldn't meet my eyes.

"All right," I said. "Whatever."

Tracy Flick

That was the last thing we needed, two football players instead of one.

Kyle Dorfman

I really didn't care about the second person. We had Vito in the bag and that was all that mattered. The second person was a footnote. But I also didn't want to sit there for the rest of the afternoon.

"I hate to say it," I said, "but it's gotta be Keezer. Whisper Girl's too weird, the Vietnam kid's dead, and no one gives a crap about the writer, so we're just gonna have to bite the bullet."

Jack Weede

I'd met Matt Keezer a few times—he was one of those unavoidable people in Green Meadow—and I couldn't stand him. You couldn't talk to the guy for five minutes without hearing about his luxury box at MetLife Stadium, or his vintage Porsche convertible. And I hated his stupid billboards; they always featured his smarmy face and a little thought bubble that said something like *Life's too short to drive a boring car* or *Get a new lease on summer.* Matt Keezer was one bullet I was not going to bite. I was just about to say so when Diane poked her head into the room, the way she always did when I had a meeting that looked like it might run a little long.

"Ten-minute warning," she said, and I couldn't believe how blind I'd been.

Tracy Flick

At first I didn't understand what Jack was up to.

"Ms. Blankenship," he said. "How long have you worked here?"

"Too long," she said. "Twenty-eight years."

"Wow." Jack gave a little whistle of surprise, though he was well aware of Diane's work history. "You must have been young when you started."

"I was twenty. Fresh out of community college."

"And you're a graduate of GMHS, correct?"

Diane shot me a puzzled glance, but all I could do was shrug.

"That's right," she said. "Class of 1986."

"And you saved a student's life? When was that, 2004?"

Diane tugged on her sweater, straightening the wrinkled snowflake.

"It wasn't a big deal." She was blushing under our collective scrutiny. "He got stung by a bee in gym class, and I guess he had a bad reaction. The nurse was out that day, so . . . I just jabbed him with an EpiPen. Anyone could've done it."

Jack nodded thoughtfully, letting that sink in for a bit.

"I've never saved anyone's life." He glanced around the room, checking in with each member of the Committee. "Have any of you ever done that?"

We all shook our heads.

"Thank you, Ms. Blankenship." Jack beamed at her—it was a sweet, boyish smile, full of affection—and I loved him in that moment. "That'll be all for now."

When Diane left, he nominated her, and we took a vote. My hand was the first in the air, but only by a fraction of a second, and it didn't matter anyway, because the Committee was unanimous.

We'd found our second person.

PART THREE:

The Overwhelming Favorite

- 18 -

Glenn Keeler needed to keep busy. That was what he always said when people asked how he managed it, working all week at his handyman business (GlennWillDoIt.com), and then volunteering his nights and weekends as an Auxiliary Police Officer, doing the thankless jobs the full-timers preferred to avoid: traffic duty, parade security, that kind of thing. Guarding a downed power line until the utility company arrived, the live wire thrashing around on the street like an angry snake, spitting out sparks. Escorting a funeral procession to the cemetery. Filling in on the graveyard shift when someone got sick at the last minute. It was all okay with Glenn.

I like to keep busy, he would say. *And I don't need a lot of sleep.*

He hated hanging around his condo at night, no one to talk to, nothing to do but stress eat, watch Fox News, and listen to the chatter on the scanner. Then it would be bedtime, and he'd be all revved up with nowhere to go. Sometimes, when his insomnia got really bad, he'd get in his Explorer and drive around for a few hours, cruising up and down the quiet streets, keeping an eye on things. The Grover PD only deployed two cars overnight, and he knew how lazy the younger guys could get. They'd idle for hours in the Wendy's parking lot, shooting the shit through their open windows, leaving the town unprotected.

It wasn't the same, patrolling in a civilian vehicle, calling in suspicious activity instead of intervening directly. But he could do it if he had to. That was why he kept a portable strobe unit mounted on his dashboard. He'd flashed it a few times, mostly at people he knew, just for fun, but once or twice with strangers whose driving he didn't like. They'd pulled right over, no hesitation whatsoever. And they'd been very respectful when he asked for their license and registration.

I'm sorry, Officer. I'll be more careful next time.

One of these days he'd get someone who wasn't so polite, some mouthy asshole with a bad attitude. And that would be fine with Glenn too, a whole different kind of fun.

Tonight was a low-stress assignment, crowd control at a basketball game between Grover and Green Meadow, Glenn's alma mater. The kids could get a little rowdy on the weekends, but he wasn't expecting any trouble on a Tuesday night. In any event, there wasn't much of a crowd—a hundred at most—because no one was expecting much of a game. The Grover Pirates were one of the best teams in the county, and the Larks were one of the worst, which was par for the course, because Green Meadow pretty much sucked at everything these days.

Glenn made a slow circuit of the bleachers before the opening tip-off, making eye contact with as many spectators as possible, scouting out potential troublemakers, letting everyone know he was on the job. They all registered his presence, even the ones who pretended not to. It was a universal truth: a cop walks by, people notice.

He would never say it out loud, but *this* was the real reason he did the job—this feeling he got, wearing the uniform in public. Normally, Glenn wasn't much to look at, an overweight middle-aged man, a little shorter than average, not much of an athlete. In a department full of bodybuilders, ex-Marines, and black belts, he was the fat guy, the one who couldn't run a mile or do twenty push-ups to save his life, which was the reason he'd never graduated from the Academy. Luckily, the standards for the Auxiliary were a little more forgiving.

The uniform improved him, though, his bulk encased by the Kevlar vest, his waistline girded by the heavy belt. He felt like the Michelin Man—armored, fully inflated, ready for anything—a force to be reckoned with. The gun was part of that, he wasn't going to deny it. He liked resting his hand on the grip, reminding himself—and everyone else—that it was there if he needed it. Some of the nearby towns had recently voted to disarm their Auxiliary Forces, but not Grover, thank God, at least not yet. If they ever took his gun away, he'd resign in a heartbeat, as painful as that would be. Without a weapon, he'd be no better than a crossing guard.

The game turned out to be more interesting than he'd expected. Green Meadow had a freshman point guard—a skinny Black kid named Marcus Turner—who'd just been brought up from jayvee. It was his first varsity game, and within five minutes, everyone could see that he was a star, playing on a whole different level than the rest of his team. He was an amazing ball handler, moving up the court in sudden explosive bursts, then stopping short and changing direction, keeping the defenders on their heels. Sometimes he'd accelerate towards the hoop; other times he'd pull up and launch a sweet three-pointer. Every now and then he'd toss an alley-oop to his tallest teammate, a clumsy giant who wore a knee brace and safety goggles. After several ugly misses, the tall kid—his name was Blake Dooley— surprised everyone by sinking three in a row. He looked so shocked and delighted when the third one went in that the whole gym started cheering, even the Grover fans.

A hand thumped against Glenn's back, hard enough to make him grunt. He whirled, instinctively covering his gun with his right hand, only to see Ralph Kingman, the former Chief of the Grover PD, looming over him with an amused grin on his face.

"Hey, Killer. Good to see you, buddy."

Glenn forced a smile, though he hated that nickname, which hardly anyone used anymore, now that Kingman had retired to Florida. The ex-Chief had stuck patronizing labels on all the Auxiliary officers—Dumbo, Hillbilly Trevor, Little Dickie. He was that kind of guy. Glenn was Killer Keeler.

"Hey, Chief," he said, out of old habit, despite the fact that Kingman wasn't Chief of Jack Shit anymore. "What brings you back to town?"

"New grandkid. Number four. Pretty soon I won't be able to keep track."

"Congratulations."

Kingman nodded his tepid thanks. He looked pretty much the same as always—same Mount Rushmore face, same salt-and-pepper crew cut, same barrel chest—just a little more sunburned from all those days on his fishing boat.

"Yeah, you gotta see the new grandkid, even in the middle of fucking January." His expression darkened. "I'll tell you, Killer. I can't take the cold anymore. Don't know how I survived all those goddam winters."

They were momentarily distracted by the sight of Marcus Turner knifing through two defenders and then spinning away from a third to score on a fadeaway jumper, nothing but net.

"Damn," said Kingman. "Kid can play. And he's even better in football. I hear he's the next Vito Falcone."

Glenn felt the name in his stomach the way he always did. *Vito Falcone.* It made him a little sick.

Kingman glanced at him. "You went to high school with Vito, right?"

"Just for a year." Glenn made an effort to sound matter-of-fact. "He was a senior when I was a freshman. My older brother was in his class."

"I used to go to all those games," Kingman said. "Vito was such a beautiful player. Best high school athlete I ever saw. Best athlete period."

Glenn did a thorough sweep of the building during halftime. A couple of years ago, some troublemakers from Riverhaven had slipped past the No Trespassing sign and spray-painted penises and profanity all over the walls; it was a real bitch to clean. As a result, the administration had sprung for a metal folding gate that locked into place, sealing off the gym area from the rest of the school.

Even so, Glenn asked Manny to open the gate so he could take a look around. When you were an Auxiliary Officer, you had to go the extra mile. He started on the second floor, checking both bathrooms, peering into every stall. It was a relief to get away from the mob swarming around the refreshment table—the proud parents, the laughing boys, the pretty girls taking pictures of themselves. Glenn didn't even want to look at their faces. He knew it was bad for a cop—this pissed-off feeling that came over him sometimes—but there was nothing he could do about it.

When he finished with the restrooms, Glenn checked all the classroom doors and supply closets, making sure everything was locked up tight. He shined his flashlight on the lockers and bulletin boards, illuminating the motivational posters lining the walls—*We Are All Amazing; Spread The Love; You Are A Valued Member Of Our Community*—and a made a small, strangled noise deep in his throat, a sound he often made when he thought of his brother.

Glenn wished he could remember Carl more clearly, but his memory had faded over the years. A few random details from their childhood had stuck in his head: Carl's insistence on eating chicken fingers and Tater Tots for every meal. His brief but passionate interest in professional wrestling. The goofy 3D glasses he liked to wear around the house.

When Carl was thirteen, he moved out of the cramped bedroom he shared with Glenn and started sleeping in the attic. He said it was because his telescope was up there and he liked to look at the stars, but it made no sense, because the attic was dusty and unfinished—freezing in the winter, stifling in the summer—with pink insulation lining the walls and a pile of dead bees in one corner.

Don't worry, their father said. *He'll come down when he's good and ready.*

But Carl never came down. He upgraded from a sleeping bag to an Army cot, and set up a folding table as a desk. He started bringing his meals up there too. At dinner it was just Glenn and his parents, as if he were an only child.

Carl had some sort of mental health crisis during the summer between his junior and senior years of high school, and had to be hospitalized for a couple of weeks. Glenn wasn't aware of this at the time because he'd been away at Boy Scout camp in the Adirondacks. It had been a life-changing experience for him, those two months in the wilderness, and it set him on the path to becoming an Eagle Scout three years later.

Carl was well enough to go back to school in September. Glenn was just starting his freshman year, and it saddened him to see his older brother drifting down the hall, always alone. He looked exactly the same as he did at home—unkempt, a little dazed, deeply worried—but it seemed worse at school, with all those other people around.

Carl never bothered anyone, so Glenn was startled, one day in late fall, to see his brother screaming at Vito Falcone in front of the sundae bar in the cafeteria. Later, Glenn would hear the whole story—Carl took too long to choose between chocolate and vanilla, and Vito tried to push in front of him—but at the time, it just felt like a weird dream, his scrawny, disheveled brother jabbing an ice cream scoop at the star quarterback, the most famous kid in the school.

You stay away! Carl's voice was higher than usual, almost a shriek. *Don't cross my boundaries!*

Vito took a lazy step backwards, raising his hands in mock surrender, as if he had no intention of crossing anyone's boundaries. He was six inches taller than Carl, and fifty pounds heavier. He looked like a grown man, like a movie star.

Whoa, he said in a soothing voice. *Take it easy.*

Carl lowered the scoop. His face was a bright, hectic red.

I'm just trying to make my sundae!

Vito smirked at his football buddies. They were gathered right behind him, a whole gang of them in their green-and-yellow varsity jackets. They'd just completed an undefeated season—the sundae bar was a gift from the Booster Club—and they were in high spirits.

You guys hear that? Vito said. *Give the man some room.*

And that was what they did. The football players stepped back and watched with exaggerated interest, murmuring their approval—*Good choice, bro*; *Gotta love the butterscotch*—as Carl clumsily assembled his dessert. To make it even worse, they gave him a polite round of applause as he headed back to his table—he always sat by himself in the back of the cafeteria—his face an even deeper shade of scarlet than before.

That should have been the end of it, but Vito grabbed a can of whipped cream and brought it over to Carl just as he was sitting down.

Dude, he said. *You forgot something.*

Carl shook his head. *I don't want any.*

No, you do, Vito insisted. *It's the most important part.*

And then he did the thing Glenn would never forgive. Vito raised the canister, pressed his finger to the nozzle, and deposited a mound of whipped cream on Carl's head.

There. Vito added one last dollop for good measure. He looked so pleased with himself. *Now you're all set.*

Carl didn't say a word, didn't even try to wipe himself off. He just picked up his spoon and started eating. Of all the memories Glenn had of his brother, that one was the most vivid: Carl trying to smile, polishing off an ice cream sundae with a crown of whipped cream on his head.

The doctors could never agree on a diagnosis—some said schizophrenia, some said bipolar, others said other things—but whatever it was, Carl got worse after high school. He dropped out of college after one semester, started medicating himself with drugs and alcohol, and wound up homeless in Manhattan, where he died of a heroin overdose at the age of twenty-four.

No one would have even known it was suicide, except that he'd taken the trouble to write a goodbye letter to his parents. It arrived in the mail a day after they'd been notified of his passing. Carl apologized for the pain and disappointment he'd caused, and explained that he'd felt like a stranger in the world—an unwanted guest—for as long as he could remember, and couldn't see that changing in the future. He asked for forgiveness, and thanked them for everything they'd done on his behalf. And then he added a little note to Glenn.

You were a good brother to me. I know it wasn't easy.

It was sweet of Carl to let him off the hook like that. But it wasn't true and they both knew it. Glenn wasn't a good brother. He could still picture himself in the cafeteria that day, watching quietly as Vito humiliated Carl in front of everyone; he didn't do a thing, he just let it happen. And when it was over, Glenn didn't confront Vito, or even bring some napkins over to Carl and help him clean up. He just sat there and ate his own lunch, one bite after another, until he cleaned his plate, and then he got up and made a sundae of his own, hot fudge with a little blob of whipped cream, and a maraschino cherry on top.

Glenn stood guard in the parking lot after the game. His last duty of the night was making sure the visiting team got safely on their bus without suffering any abuse or harassment. The Green Meadow kids looked pretty glum as they trudged out of the locker room—despite Marcus Turner's stellar performance, they'd ended up losing by twenty points. Glenn gave a fist bump and offered a kind word to each of them as they climbed aboard.

"Good game . . . Way to go . . . You'll get 'em next time."

He was extra nice to Blake Dooley, who'd had a rough second half.

"Good job." Glenn craned his neck to meet the tall kid's eyes. "You made some terrific shots out there."

Blake muttered his thanks and stepped onto the bus. Marcus Turner was next. Bundled in his winter coat, he looked younger than he had on the court, a lot less fierce. He paused after the fist bump, waiting to be told how great he was.

Glenn hesitated. He wanted to say, *Don't be a dick like Vito Falcone. Treat other people with respect. You're not better than anyone else.* But the words stayed in his throat.

"Great game tonight," he said. "Really outstanding."

Marcus nodded, accepting his due. There were a few more Green Meadow kids after that, and then the bus drove away, white smoke pouring from the exhaust pipe. When it was out of sight, Glenn did a few jumping jacks in the empty parking lot, warming himself up, killing a little time, wishing there were someplace to go besides home.

- 19 -

Tracy Flick

I've never done any online dating—it seems like a terrible idea for a woman in the public eye—but I've heard numerous colleagues complain about how exhausting it can be, meeting stranger after stranger, serving yourself up like the daily special, and then somehow finding the energy and optimism to do it all over again with the next person in line.

You want to know what's a hundred times worse? Interviewing to be a high school Principal. If a date doesn't work out, you've only lost a few hours of your time. But the interview process can stretch out for months, requiring you to jump through multiple hoops as you advance from one round to the next. And there are so many people involved in the vetting process—parents, the School Board, politicians, curriculum specialists, paraprofessionals, and on and on—you never really know who's making the decisions, what kinds of discussions are going on behind closed doors, or even whether an entire job search is a sham with a foregone conclusion. It's possible to do everything right—impress the stakeholders, wow the Admin Team, nail the budget analysis—and still come up empty-handed.

Believe me, I've been there. By the time I was interviewing to be Jack Weede's successor at GMHS, I'd already been a finalist to lead three other high schools. I guess you could look on the bright side and say, *Hey, that's pretty good, you're clearly a viable candidate, it's only a matter of time until you land the top job and get your chance to shine*, and sometimes I was able to do that, to maintain a positive attitude and a healthy sense of perspective. But I'd be lying if I said that every one of those defeats didn't take something out of me. They undermined my confidence, sapped my energy, and damaged my reputation.

All the jobs I'd competed for were within half an hour of Green Meadow, and word got around. My prospective employers checked references and made phone calls, and some of them even visited GMHS to speak directly to my colleagues and supervisors. So everyone in the local education community knew that I was looking to ascend to the next level, which meant they also knew that I'd failed to achieve my goal, because there I was, still the Assistant Principal, Jack Weede's loyal sidekick. Once that happens a few times, you start to get that stink on you—the stink of the runner-up, the also-ran, the perennial bridesmaid. If you're not careful, it can become your signature odor, your very own personal scent.

Eau de Loser.

Coming in second too many times is tough on anyone's self-esteem, but it was especially hard for me, because it brought back memories I'd prefer not to dwell on. Back when I was in high school, I lost an election for President of the Student Government Association because a teacher—our civics instructor, if you can believe that— tampered with the votes.

It sounds crazy, but it's true. This crooked teacher—a man I'd liked and respected and learned a lot from—wanted my male opponent to win so badly, he tossed two ballots into the trash, turning me from a winner into a loser. That's how close it was—I won by a single vote— which was humiliating in and of itself, because I was so overqualified for the job it was ridiculous. I'd been preparing to run for President ever since middle school, and probably even before that. I'd climbed my way methodically up the ladder of Student Government— Homeroom Representative as a freshman, Secretary the following year

(highly unusual for a sophomore), and then Treasurer as a junior—
putting in the time, doing the work, earning the trust of my fellow
students. Or at least I thought so, until half of them stabbed me in the
back by voting for my completely unqualified but super-popular rival.

For a while, in my twenties, I tried to turn it into a funny story,
but no one ever laughed. I think it just made people wonder if there
was something wrong with me, and I couldn't help wondering that
myself, because why else would a teacher hate me so much that he'd
ruin his life just to stop me from getting something I desperately
wanted and totally deserved?

In the end, the fraud was exposed. The teacher resigned and I
became President, but my victory never felt as good or as clean as it
should have. The whole experience left a bad taste in my mouth that
still hasn't gone away, and I doubt it ever will.

That said, things appeared to be looking pretty good on the GMHS
front. Kyle had told me back in August that I was the overwhelming
favorite, and it still felt that way at the beginning of February. My
first-round interview had been a lovefest, one softball question after
another lobbed at me by a large and diverse panel of friendly faces.
I made the case for a Flick administration, strategically distancing
myself from Jack without throwing him under the bus, or casting a
shadow on my own performance as Assistant Principal. It's not an
easy tightrope to walk—just ask Al Gore—but I thought I handled
it pretty well, promising new energy and a shift in emphasis, rather
than a wholesale change in direction.

It was refreshing to find myself on the inside track for once, talking to people who already knew me, and had firsthand experience
of my leadership capabilities. They understood how much of Jack's
workload had been shifted onto my shoulders in recent years, and
they'd seen me run the school for a semester and a half while he was
recovering from his heart attack. During my tenure as Acting Principal, GMHS hadn't missed a step. If anything, we'd done a little

better than usual, showing small but significant improvements on test scores and various metrics of student satisfaction. I made sure to downplay my responsibility for these good outcomes—though I also made sure to mention them every chance I got—which earned me points (I hoped) for modesty as well as competence.

The first sign that something was amiss came in my second-round, one-on-one interview with the Superintendent of Schools. I went into it feeling cautiously optimistic. After all, Buzz Bramwell had hired me at GMHS, and he'd never expressed anything but satisfaction with my work.

As soon as I arrived at the Admin Building, though, I could sense that something was off. Buzz kept me waiting for fifteen minutes, and didn't apologize when his secretary finally admitted me into his office.

"Dr. Flick," he said, without even a trace of a smile. "Thank you for coming."

No *Tracy.* No *Nice to see you.* All business.

"I'm happy to be here, Dr. Bramwell." Normally I would have called him Buzz, but it felt safer to mirror his formality. "I appreciate the opportunity."

"So," he said. "I hear you were a big hit with the stakeholders."

"It was a friendly crowd. But they asked some tough questions."

He nodded judiciously, not so much in agreement with me as with some private hypothesis of his own. Buzz was maybe five foot four, bald and boyish at the same time. He was meticulously dressed as always—tweed three-piece suit and a plaid bow tie—and he had an air of dignity and quiet authority I'd always admired.

"I'm sure they did," he told me. "And I'm sure you handled them without a hitch. You're very quick on your feet."

His tone was matter-of-fact, but I thought I detected a hint of criticism, as if being quick on my feet was a character flaw, a sign of shiftiness or opportunism rather than a virtue.

"Thank you," I said. "It was a very productive dialogue."

He removed his round rimless eyeglasses, sprayed the lenses with fluid from a small pump bottle, and wiped them clean with a shiny cloth.

"Principal's a big step up," he observed, guiding the glasses back into place, taking a moment to balance them properly on the bridge of his nose. "What makes you think you're ready?"

This struck me as a patronizing question, considering that I'd already done the job, but I kept my poker face.

"I've paid my dues," I told him. "I've learned a lot from Jack Weede, and from you, and I've formed strong working relationships throughout the building. With all due respect, I believe I'm the most qualified person to lead Green Meadow High School into the twenty-first century."

"I've got some news for you, Dr. Flick. We're already there."

"The world is," I countered. "But our school is lagging behind. We have some catching up to do."

"I don't disagree." He made a micro-adjustment to his bow tie. "Can you give me some specifics?"

I started in the obvious place, drilling down on our deficiencies in STEM subjects, and computer science in particular. It wasn't just a matter of upgrading our hardware. The deeper problem was the CS faculty, none of whom had real-world experience in the tech sector, or genuine expertise in the subject. Our advanced students knew a lot more about coding, 3D printing, and computer graphics than our teachers did.

"Maybe that was forgivable twenty years ago when Kyle Dorfman was a teenager, but at this point it's a travesty that—"

He held up his hand to silence me.

"You know what, Tracy?" He sounded annoyed. "Why don't we leave Kyle out of it?"

"I was just using him as an example—"

"Mr. Dorfman's not here," he said. "It's just you and me. Two professionals." He gave me a tight, unfriendly smile. "Please continue."

I took a breath and forced myself back into the moment. Something weird had just happened, something I'd have to ponder later on, but right then I needed to focus on the interview. I couldn't afford to get rattled.

"It's not just a STEM problem, Dr. Bramwell. It's an across-the-board issue in our Honors and AP classes. We have a number of veteran teachers who've gotten lazy and complacent, and it's a disservice to our students. That's going to change if I'm in charge. I don't care if you have tenure, or if you were Teacher of the Year in 2008, or all the kids think you're funny and cool. If you're not working up to your potential, if you're not taking concrete, measurable steps to expand your knowledge base and upgrade your skill set, you're going to have to answer to me. No more phoning it in. Not on my watch."

"Tell that to the teachers' union."

"I already have. And they didn't like it. But if I'm Principal, maybe they'll start to listen. Especially if the Superintendent has my back."

He considered this for a moment, trying to decide whether he was offended.

"If you're the Principal, you can rest assured that I'll have your back. But here's the thing, Tracy. I want our schools to work for all of our students, not just the high achievers."

"I do too. That's exactly what—"

"You say that, but all you ever talk about is the top kids. AP this and Ivy League that. It's the same with your buddy Kyle and his Hall of Fame."

"My what? He's not my—"

"It's just a covert form of elitism." His face was placid but he sounded upset. "Another way of saying that some people matter more than others—the star athletes and the computer geniuses and the rich guys. You know what, though? The high achievers are going to be fine regardless. It's the other kids who need our help. The ones who are struggling, who maybe don't have all the advantages. We have to serve all our students equally, including the losers and slackers and the kids with special needs. I want a Principal who shares that agenda. Otherwise we're at cross-purposes, you and me, and that's not going to help anyone."

I shook my head, trying to ignore the clammy sweat pooling in the small of my back.

"We're not at cross-purposes," I assured him. "Not even with the Hall of Fame. I voted for Front Desk Diane. She doesn't even have a bachelor's degree." I should have stopped there, but I couldn't help myself. "And if you think I give a crap about Vito Falcone, you're sorely mistaken."

For the first time since I'd arrived, he cracked a smile. "Not a big football fan, are you, Tracy?"

"Not really," I said. "It's a stupid game."

I wanted the words back as soon as they were out of my mouth.

"Good to know," he said. "I appreciate your honesty."

The rest of the interview was uneventful. Buzz and I parted on cordial terms, and I went back to work and did my best to put it out of my mind. Usually I'm pretty good at that—moving forward, focusing on the task at hand—because you have to be, if you're going to accomplish anything in this world. The past is always looking over your shoulder, whispering things you don't want to hear. You just have to ignore it until it goes away.

- 20 -

Jack Weede

The *Messenger* article came out in early February: *Football Hero, Office Worker Tapped for Kudos.* It was poorly written —no surprises there—and riddled with factual errors. Vito was said to be a first-round NFL draft pick (he was actually chosen in the second), and his knee injury was misstated as a broken leg. At least the quote attributed to me was accurate: "Diane Blankenship has served the GMHS community for nearly three decades with exceptional loyalty and exemplary competence. She is universally beloved by our staff and students, and my personal gratitude towards her is immense. She is deeply deserving of this wonderful honor."

The article instantly transformed the GMHS Hall of Fame from a rumor to a reality. It included the date for the Induction Ceremony—mid-March, right around the corner—and information about ticket sales. The whole school was buzzing about it, students and faculty stopping by the main office to congratulate Diane and jokingly ask for her autograph. People were genuinely excited about her selection. It made sense. She was an underdog—a woman, a local resident, an ordinary person—the perfect foil to Vito Falcone. If Front Desk Diane could make it into the Hall of Fame, maybe there was hope for all of us.

She was glowing that afternoon when she knocked on my office door, standing up straight and tall, like a neglected plant that had finally gotten some water and sunshine.

"I just wanted to thank you for what you said in the paper. It was very kind of you."

"It was nothing," I told her. "The least I could do."

She smiled, a little sadly, and we shared one of those complicated looks you can only exchange with someone who knows all your secrets, someone you used to love.

"If I'd known how much fun it was to be famous," she said, "I would've done it a long time ago."

I drove home that night feeling pretty good about myself.

It was gratifying, being able to do something nice for Diane before I retired. She deserved it, and it made my burden of guilt just a little bit lighter. I didn't plan it out or think it through; I just saw an opportunity and grabbed it, and it had all worked out for the best.

Or so I thought, right up to the moment when I stepped into my house. Normally I would have been greeted by the sound of the radio, the earnest voices on NPR, and the inviting smell of dinner on the stove. But that evening there was only a chilly, ominous silence.

Alice was waiting for me in the kitchen, her face puffy, her eyes raw from crying. There was a mostly empty bottle of wine on the table, resting on the front page of the *Messenger*, next to the photos of Vito and Diane.

"I guess she was really good in bed, huh?"

"What are you talking about?"

"Your *mistress*," she said. "Does she have some special talent or something?"

I wanted to play dumb, but there wasn't any point. I already knew what they felt like, those old mobsters on the TV news, dragged out of bed and handcuffed in their bathrobes, arrested for crimes they could barely even remember, the idiots who thought they'd gotten away with it.

"You bastard," she said. "You put her in the Hall of Fame?"

- 21 -

Lily Chu

My parents let me go to Wesleyan for the weekend. I presented it to them as a "college visit," and that was true enough—Wesleyan was one of the many schools I had applied to, and it had moved up on my list since Cornell rejected my Early Decision app in December.

"It's very highly ranked," I assured them over dinner. "I mean, it's not technically an Ivy, but it's really close. And I can stay with my friend from Girls' Code Camp. It's all worked out."

My mother studied me a little too closely. She'd been doing that a lot lately. "Which friend is this?"

"Clem. I told you about Clem."

"What's her last name?"

"Clemmons."

"Clem Clemmons?"

"No. Her first name's Amelia, but she prefers Clem."

I wanted to use the right pronouns, but this didn't seem like the best time. My parents were pretty strict, and neither one of them spoke English as their first language. There were a lot of reasons they weren't going to like the singular form of *they/them*.

"Where will you sleep?" my father asked.

"There's a couch in the living room. Clem has two other room-mates."

"Girls?"

I nodded, and my father gave me a stern look.

"No drinking," he said.

"No drinking," I promised.

"And no frat parties."

"You really don't have to worry about that."

It would have been a lot faster to drive to Middletown, but my parents didn't think I had enough highway experience, so I had to take a train to Penn Station, a cab to Grand Central, and then another train to New Haven. Clem borrowed a car from a friend and met me at the station.

We hadn't seen each other in person for six months, and I was a little scared when I entered the terminal, like maybe the magic would be gone, and we wouldn't know what to say to each other, or how to act. But then I spotted them—they were standing by the benches, holding a bouquet of flowers, with the sweetest crooked smile on their face—and we didn't even say hello. We just started making out right there, in front of all those people, and that kind of set the tone for the whole weekend.

Nate Cleary

I haven't seen a lot of famous people in real life. I was with my dad once in New York City—I was maybe ten years old—and he stopped in his tracks, spun around, and said, *Holy shit, that's Annette Bening!* I could tell it was a big deal, though I'd never even heard the name before. A few years after that, I spotted Vince Vaughn in an airport; he was just standing there, talking on the phone. He was hard to miss, because he's really tall. On a school trip to DC my junior year, I had to step aside to make way for Dr. Sanjay Gupta, who was exiting the men's room at a rest area on the New Jersey Turnpike. That was the weirdest, because I couldn't help thinking that if I'd gotten there a minute earlier, I might've found myself standing next to Dr. Gupta at a urinal, though I guess it's possible that he uses a stall for privacy, even when he pees. That's what I would do if I ever became famous.

My point is this: it takes a second or two before you realize you're looking at a celebrity. At first, it just feels normal, like, *Hey, I know you,* but then you're like, *Wait, do I?* And then it hits you, this delayed jolt of adrenaline that tells you something special just occurred, something you'll remember for the rest of your life.

That's what happened to me in Starbucks. It was a Tuesday night, and there were maybe like ten people in there, including a blond girl working on a laptop. I gave her a quick glance as I headed towards the counter, and then I stopped in my tracks and looked again.

Holy shit, I thought. *That's Kelly Harbaugh!*

Lily Chu

I liked what I saw of Wesleyan, though I didn't see as much of it as I probably should have. Mostly we stayed in Clem's room, tangled together on that skinny little bed, though we did go to the dining hall for Saturday brunch, and to an off-campus party that night. They introduced me to some of their friends—*This is my girlfriend, Lily*—and we danced for a little while, but we decided to skip out early, because the weekend was flying by so fast and we wanted to make the most of every single minute.

We stayed up talking the whole night, filling in the details of our life stories, every little thing we could think of. It was so amazing to be reunited—to be able to kiss them again, to feel their arms around me, to run my hand over their stubbly hair—but it was sad too, because our time was almost up, and we were just getting started.

"This is too good," Clem told me. "I don't want to go back to FaceTime."

"Me neither."

"When can you visit again?"

"Probably not for a while. My mom's already suspicious."

Clem knew I needed to keep our relationship a secret. They'd been in the exact same position when they were my age.

"Maybe I could visit you," they said. "Over my spring break. I could come for a whole week if you want."

"Oh God," I said. "That would be so weird."

"We don't have to sleep in the same bed or anything. We can just say we're friends."

I wanted them to visit, to show them around Green Meadow,

to hold hands and make out in Monroe Park. But I couldn't quite imagine Clem and my parents under the same roof.

"They think you're a girl named Amelia," I said.

"That's okay," they told me. "My parents think the exact same thing."

Nate Cleary

I had to walk right past Kelly to get to my table.

"Nate?" she said. "Is that you?"

I did that little dance where you stop short and blink a couple of times, and pretend you didn't recognize the person.

"Oh, wow. Kelly. Hey. How's it going?"

"Not bad." She bobbed her head from side to side. "I'm taking some time off from school. Just moved back home with my parents. What are you, a senior now?"

"Yeah. It's my last semester."

"Fun times."

"I wish. I don't know where I'm going to college, and I'm way behind on my thesis. It's pretty stressful."

She was dressed super casual—Uggs, plaid pajama pants, a big Rutgers hoodie—but she had a full coat of makeup on her face, and pink polish on her fingernails.

"You need to chill," she said. "You were always kind of a worrier. Even back in summer camp."

"You remember that?"

"How could I forget? We were the chicken fight champs." She nodded at the empty chair across from her. "Wanna sit down?"

It felt a little unreal, as if Vince Vaughn had invited me to hang out with him in the first-class lounge.

"You sure?"

She gave me a look, like, *Don't be a weirdo, dude.*

So I sat and we started talking about people we knew, the colleges I applied to, stuff like that. I'd always thought of her as so much older than me, so much more together, but it didn't feel that way anymore. It felt like we were pretty much in the same place in our lives—stuck in Green Meadow, waiting for the next thing to happen—except I also knew that we weren't, and finally I couldn't help myself.

"Just so you know," I said. "I'm a big fan of your videos."

She was surprised that I even knew about them—I didn't look like someone who watched a lot of makeup tutorials—so I had to explain the whole Hall of Fame thing: Kyle, the Committee, Vito Falcone, Front Desk Diane. It was all news to her. She didn't even know she'd been nominated, and was deeply relieved to hear that she hadn't been chosen. When I asked why, she looked at me like I was a fool.

"Do you ever read the comments?"

"Some of them," I said. "People really like you."

"There are so many creeps out there." She hunched her shoulders and gave a little shudder of disgust. "Soooo many creeps. I don't want them to know my real name. I don't want them coming to my *house*."

For a second or two, I thought about mentioning that I'd voted against her, like maybe she'd be grateful for that, or think it was funny, but then I reconsidered. There was no point in dredging up the past, confessing to a stupid grudge I'd been holding since freshman year. That was a long time ago. We were both different people now.

"I don't care about the makeup," I said. "I just like the way you whisper. And that thing you do with your fingernails. That's pretty cool too."

"This?" She did a little *Tap Tap Tap* for me on the tabletop. "That's my signature."

I wanted to tell her that I liked the way she licked her lips too, but that seemed like it might be edging into the creep zone, so I kept it to myself, which turned out to be the right move. We talked until closing time, and then she wrote her cell number on the back of my hand, and told me to text her if I ever felt like hanging out.

- 22 -

Tracy Flick

For several days after my interview, I was dogged by a feeling of unease, a sense—a premonition almost—that in spite of all my hard work and meticulous preparation, I might be headed for another defeat. Why else would Buzz have treated me like an adversary? I'd assumed he was on my side, not only because he liked me and respected my work, but because Kyle and the Board were on my side, and Buzz supposedly followed their lead: *He doesn't wipe his ass without Board approval.* Either Kyle was wrong about that, or Buzz knew something I didn't about the Board's actual preferences.

I got so anxious I called Kyle at home—something I'd never done before—to let him know what had happened and feel him out about my prospects. He didn't seem too concerned.

"Buzz is a prickly character," he said. "He likes to make a big show of independence before he falls in line. It's the only way he can salvage some self-respect."

"So there's nothing going on that I need to . . . ?"

"Stop worrying, Tracy. Everything's fine."

"Okay. *Phew.*" I felt my abs loosen a little. "I mean, for him to accuse me of *elitism*—it's so unfair. I was raised by a single mom. We had *nothing.* I went to college on a scholarship. I worked and scraped for everything I ever got. I'm the exact opposite of an elitist."

Kyle grunted in amusement. "You know what an elitist is? It's just

163

someone who—" He stopped abruptly, and I heard some mumbling on the other end of the line. "Hold on, Tracy. Marissa wants to talk to you."

"Wait," I said, because I wanted to hear Kyle's definition of an elitist, but he'd already handed over the phone.

"Hey you." Marissa's voice was bright and familiar in my ear. "How've you been?"

"Not bad. Little busy."

"Tell me about it. Listen, I know this is short notice, but Kyle's taking the boys skiing this weekend, and I'm just hanging out on my own. If you're free on Saturday night, I thought maybe we could have a glass of wine at my place, maybe go in the sauna if we feel like it. It's up on the roof. It's pretty cozy on a winter night."

"Oh, wow. That's so nice of you. But I have my daughter this weekend. I'm sorry."

"Okay." She didn't sound too upset. "Guess I'll just have to drink alone. Have a good night."

"You too."

I felt a little embarrassed when the call was over. It wasn't actually my weekend with Sophia, and I had nothing planned for Saturday night. I'd used my daughter as an excuse, because it was easier than telling Marissa the truth, which was that I'd gotten out of the habit of making friends, and preferred to be alone, or maybe I'd never gotten into the habit in the first place.

- 23 -

Vito didn't believe in love at first sight. He wasn't even sure he believed in love period, though he'd said, *I love you* multiple times to all three of his wives—usually after they'd said it to him, but still—and to a few other women as well. It was part of the script, a phrase that needed to be uttered every now and again. Not a lie, exactly, more like a Hallmark card, a good thing you wanted to be true, like *Number One Dad* or *The Most Wonderful Time of the Year.* People liked when you said it, and they got upset when you didn't, so why not throw them the bone?

So no, he wasn't prepared to call it love at first sight. But it had been *something*, that jolt he felt when Paige walked into the basement of Holy Redeemer and took her seat in the Tuesday-night circle. She was pretty, that was part of it—she had a girl-next-door quality that he liked, a healthy glow that seemed out of place in that room full of slumped shoulders and worried faces—but it went deeper than that, the sense of recognition, or maybe relief, that washed over him, as if he'd been waiting for something for a long time, and now the wait was over. She seemed to sense it too, because she looked right back and held his gaze, but not in a flirty or playful way, because she was past all that and wanted him to know it right from the start.

Everybody at the meetings had a bad story to tell; that was why they were there. Paige's wasn't the worst, not even close. She'd been a party girl in college, a weekend binge drinker. There'd been a few blackouts, and more than a few regrettable hookups, but on balance, the fun outweighed the mess, all the way through her twenties. It wasn't until she got married and had a couple of kids that she began to realize she had a problem. It was hard to admit, because she had an enviable life—her husband was ten years older, a Certified Financial Planner; they had a nice house, nice cars, a pool, all the goodies—but she was bored out of her skull, and she drank to take the edge off. At least that was what she told herself.

It was the opposite of bingeing. A little at breakfast, a little after yoga class, a sip or two at lunch, a few slugs while sitting with the other parents in the waiting area of Karate Mike's Academy of Self-Defense, where it seemed like she spent half her life. Mostly it was vodka in the travel mug that was her constant companion. People teased her for being a coffee addict, and she was happy to encourage them. She got a lot of Starbucks gift cards at Christmastime.

One day she was running late after school, hurrying to get her kids to the dojo. She took a corner too fast, swerved to avoid a kid on a bike, and ended up plowing across a neighbor's lawn, no casualties except an ornamental lemon tree and the front bumper of her SUV.

"I'd give you the gory details," she said, "but you can just google 'Obnoxious Drunk Driving Yoga Mom' and watch the whole thing on YouTube. Then you can hate me like everybody else."

There were murmurs of recognition from the circle. Apparently the video of her arrest had gone viral back in the fall. Vito had missed it at the time—he'd been distracted by his own problems—but he checked it out as soon as he got home.

The footage started after the accident had occurred, and a crowd of neighborhood busybodies had gathered to watch the fun. Paige was arguing with a pair of cops—she was wearing yoga clothes and a Marlins cap with her blond ponytail sticking out the back—and her two kids were standing nearby, looking stunned and teary-eyed in their karate outfits.

She didn't resist when they cuffed her and walked her past the crowd to the patrol car. She just kept smiling and shaking her head, acting like the whole thing was a stupid misunderstanding. Then she stopped and turned towards the onlookers.

"Suck my dick," she said in a cheerful voice. "All you assholes can suck my dick."

"That's nice," a woman yelled. "Nice example for your kids."

"Eat shit," Paige replied as they ducked her into the patrol car. "I'm a good mother."

A million and a half people had watched the video. The comments were brutal. They said she should rot in jail for the rest of her life. Her kids should be taken away. She was a disgusting foul-mouthed bitch who might as well kill herself. She was the whitest white woman in the world, an embodiment of everything that was wrong with America, and she had no business wearing those yoga pants, not with that fat ass of hers.

Vito watched the clip three times, and it didn't make him hate her. It just made him wish he had her phone number so he could call and tell her it would be okay, that everybody made mistakes, that all you could do was apologize to the people you'd hurt and try to be a better person in the future. He also wanted to tell her that he liked the way she looked in her yoga clothes, and that he'd laughed out loud when she told those assholes to suck her dick.

It got serious pretty quickly. They went to the same meetings on Tuesdays, Thursdays, and Fridays, and he was always happy to give her a ride home—her license had been revoked—and happy to follow her upstairs, into that little one-bedroom apartment that was almost as depressing as his own, though it had been decorated with a lot more care. There were fresh flowers on the kitchen table—Vito always reminded himself to send her a bouquet, though he never followed through—and the pastel sheets on her bed were clean and cool. He slept better when she was next to him.

It wasn't always fun, though. She cried a lot, missed her kids so much it was like a physical illness. For the time being, she was only allowed to see them once a week—just a few hours on Sunday afternoons, in the house she'd been banished from—and it always took her a few days to recover. Vito was patient with her—one thing he'd learned over the past few months was patience—and he discovered that comforting her eased his own pain, or at least kept him from dwelling on it so much.

Wesley told him it was a bad idea, throwing himself into a new relationship, especially with another person in the early stages of recovery. He advised Vito to concentrate on his own sobriety and let Paige do the same. Love affairs could be stressful, he explained, and often triggered relapses.

"Keep it simple," he said. "Don't get distracted."

"I hear you," Vito said. "But I think Paige and I can help each other."

"A lot of people think like that," Wesley told him. "And most of them are wrong."

Vito didn't speak up very often at the meetings, but he wanted Paige to hear his story. There were some things he hadn't been able to tell her when they were alone, things she deserved to know. So he took the floor one night in February and made his confession.

He talked about his disappointing career in the NFL, his bad marriages, his headaches and memory problems, the fear that he'd damaged his brain and was drifting into oblivion. He talked about his fragile ego, and the way the bourbon had puffed it up, reminding him of who he used to be, the charming asshole with talent to burn, the guy who always got the girls, the adulation, the money, everything he wanted.

"But I'm not that guy," he said. "Not anymore. I'm a drunk, a bad husband, a terrible father. I hit my wife in front of my kids and I can't take that back. I'm scared that when I'm dead, that's all they're gonna remember about me. So that's what I'm dealing with right now. It's heavy, I'm not gonna lie. Coming to these meetings helps a lot, though. Knowing we're all in the same boat, helping each other. That's what keeps me going."

Paige was quiet on the way home. He wondered if she was having second thoughts now that she knew the worst. He wouldn't blame her if she did.

"You . . . still want me to come up?" he asked, when they got back to her place.

"Yeah," she said. "Why wouldn't I?"

They didn't have sex that night. Paige turned off the light and they lay there for a while, wide awake in the dark.

"Do you still get the headaches?" she asked.

"Sometimes," he said. "Not so much lately. And my memory's a little better now that I stopped drinking. But something's not right. I can feel it."

"Maybe you should see a doctor. A neurologist or . . ."

Vito wasn't sure he wanted a diagnosis—in some ways, it was better not to know—and from what he'd heard, the doctors couldn't always tell, not while you were still alive.

"I will," he said. "If it starts getting bad again."

She took his hand under the covers and gave it a squeeze.

"I wish I could've seen you play."

He had some DVDs he could show her. High school scouting footage. College highlights. The four games he'd started as a Dolphin, before his fucking knee blew out. He watched them sometimes when he needed a boost, to remind himself of what that had felt like, though it didn't always work.

"I meant to tell you," he said. "I got invited back to my hometown. They're putting me in the high school Hall of Fame. There's a ceremony next month."

"Really?" she said. "That's so cool. Good for you."

It was cool, in a small-time kind of way. At the same time, he had mixed feelings about returning to Green Meadow, a place he'd avoided for years. There were some good memories back there, but there were a lot of bad ones too.

"You want to come with me?" he asked, surprising both of them.

"Are you kidding?" she said. "I would love that."

- 24 -

Kyle Dorfman

I'll admit it.

I made a mistake back in August when I told Tracy she was a shoo-in for the Principal job. I was laser focused on getting her support for the Hall of Fame, and it's possible I wasn't as careful with my language as I should have been. She was in a strong position, there was no doubt about that, but it wasn't a done deal, and I shouldn't have suggested that it was.

The thing is, a job search like that can take on a life of its own. There was a lot of enthusiasm for Tracy at the beginning of the process, but it turned out to be weak and qualified. Everyone respected her, but no one *loved* her. Aside from me, no one even liked her that much. She had no champions, no one who was willing to go to the mat on her behalf, to insist that she was the one and only.

There was an undercurrent in all of the Board's deliberations, unspoken but clearly present: *Maybe it doesn't have to be her; maybe we can do better.* Maybe there's a challenger out there, a fresh face who might be a little more inspiring, a little more creative and unpredictable. Someone who could shake things up, get us moving in a new direction. I knew this because I felt it strongly myself. Disruption was my brand; mavericks were my people.

The problem was, we didn't have a lot of mavericks applying to be Principal of GMHS. Most of the candidates were veteran educators, careerists who had worked their way through the ranks and were looking to step up to the top job. They were fine as far as they went, but there was no reason to prefer any of them to Tracy.

Angela Vargas was her only competition. Dr. Vargas was a rising star, a thirty-two-year-old charter school administrator from Paterson with a stellar résumé—Columbia Teachers College, Fulbright Scholar, fluent in Spanish and conversant in Arabic—and a sheaf of over-the-top recommendations. She was full of big ideas in her first-round interview, advocating for girls-only STEM classes and a later start to the school day, and she provoked strong reactions from the Board. Kitty Valvanos thought she was by far the most impressive candidate we'd seen, while Ricky Pizzoli accused the rest of us of going easy on her in the Q&A because she was a woman of color. This angered Charisse Turner, who pointed out that Ricky had never once complained about any of the white people who'd been given passes over the years.

I wasn't as enthusiastic as some of my colleagues. Having spent my professional life in Silicon Valley, I had reservations about the single-sex classes—I thought they would backfire on our female students, leaving them ill-prepared for the male-dominated tech world—but I was open to persuasion, eager to hear more. Unfortunately, Dr. Vargas withdrew from the process the day before her second-round interview, informing us via email that she'd accepted a position with a prestigious private foundation that paid twice what we were offering.

So that was that. By the end of February, Tracy was back on top. We'd done our due diligence, considered all the viable alternatives, and ended up right where we started, with our very own highly capable, perfectly acceptable Assistant Principal.

And then I got a call from Buzz Bramwell on a Thursday night, asking if I was free for dinner on Saturday.

"Just you," he said. "Not your spouse. There's some confidential business we need to discuss."

Tracy Flick

I have to give Marissa credit for tenacity. If I were her, I would have given up, but she reached out for the third time on the Friday after Valentine's Day.

"Hey there," she said. "It's your favorite stalker."

"Hey," I said. "How's it going?"

I was happy to hear her voice. I'd been having a rough week—anxiety about the job search, difficulty meditating, winter malaise, you name it. Also, my nose had been bleeding, something that hadn't happened since college, when it had been really bad. I'd gotten both nostrils cauterized senior year, and that had solved the problem—permanently, I thought. But in the past few days, out of nowhere, it had started up again with a vengeance. At the office. In my car. At the dinner table. I'd be going about my business, and my nose would erupt. It was gross and embarrassing.

"Do you have a cold?" she asked. "You sound a little congested."

"No. I've got a wad of toilet paper shoved up my left nostril. Bloody nose."

"Ugh. My son Ike gets those. You should swab some Vaseline inside your nasal passages. That helps sometimes."

"Yeah, I know all the tricks."

"Do you have a humidifier?"

"I used to. It broke last year."

"I think we have an extra. Let me check the basement."

"You really don't have to do that."

She was quiet for a second or two, letting me know that we were done with the nosebleed portion of the conversation.

"So listen," she said, already sounding a little doubtful. "I know it's last minute, but Kyle's going out tomorrow, and the boys have a sleepover, so I'm on my own again, if you're . . ."

She left it there, more of a vague hope than an invitation. I felt that familiar reflex kicking in—*just say no and be left alone*—but I ignored it. I was tired of being left alone.

"Sure," I said. "That would be great."

"Really?" She didn't try to hide her surprise. "Wow . . . okay . . . you want to come here? Seven thirty?"

"That's fine."

"You can bring a bathing suit if you want. In case we feel like going in the sauna. No pressure, though. Only if you feel comfortable."

"No worries," I said. "I'll bring a suit."

I actually had to go out on Saturday afternoon and buy a new one. My Speedo tank was fifteen years old, a relic from a time when I'd injured my knee and needed to take a break from running. I swam laps at the Y three or four mornings a week for six months and hated every minute of it. The suit still fit, but it was saggy in some places and threadbare in others, not the impression I wanted to make.

I felt weirdly optimistic all day, excited by the break in my routine, relief from the February tedium. I could hear my mother's voice echoing in my head: *See, honey. It's not that hard. You just have to get out of your comfort zone.* That feeling lasted all through the day and into the evening, right up to the moment when I pulled into the driveway, next to Kyle's big red Tesla, and realized that I'd made a mistake.

You don't belong here.

It was a moonless night, and that ridiculous house was glowing like some kind of alien space station—there were multiple spotlights shining on it from the front yard—and I couldn't imagine what Marissa and I would talk about for the next two hours, or however long it would take for me to extricate myself without seeming rude. I considered the possibility of backing out, texting her that I wasn't feeling well, but just then the front door opened and Kyle emerged, wearing an unbuttoned overcoat and a long striped scarf. He squinted in my direction, then raised his hand in a tentative greeting. I had no choice but to get out of the car and meet him on the curving slate path that connected the driveway to the house.

"Tracy," he said, releasing me from an unexpected and slightly awkward hug. "I'm so bummed I can't hang out with you tonight. I've got this annoying dinner thing."

"That's okay. Maybe some other time."

"I hope so." His face brightened. "By the way, I went to Royal Trophy last week, and they did a beautiful job with the plaques. They look just like the ones in Cooperstown, especially Vito's. Quality work. All that's left is the engraving, so we're right on schedule for the ceremony."

"That's a relief."

He nodded in satisfaction, and gave me a brotherly pat on the shoulder.

"You know what?" he said. "We might just pull this thing off."

Kyle Dorfman

I thought it would just be me and Buzz at the Casa de Pamplona, so I was surprised to see that Ricky Pizzoli and Charisse Turner had also been invited.

"I didn't realize it was a Board meeting," I said, sliding into the leatherette booth next to Charisse. "Are Kitty and Andrea coming too?"

"It's not an official meeting," Buzz assured me. "Just a friendly little gathering."

I glanced at my colleagues, expecting to see amusement on their faces—Ricky and Charisse were about as friendly with each other as I was with Buzz—but they were both nodding in solemn agreement, as if a profound truth had been spoken.

Tracy Flick

Marissa greeted me at the door with a bulky white box in her arms. It had a piece of paper taped to the front that read <u>TRACY—PLEASE REMEMBER!</u> The words were written in blue marker, underlined in black, and circled in red.

"This is your humidifier," she told me. "I'm just gonna leave it here by the door so we don't forget." She set the box on the floor. "We're not gonna forget, right?"

"Thanks," I said. "That's really kind of you."

"No big deal." She straightened up and gave me a quick hug, brushing her cheek against mine. "Is it cold out? Your face is cold."

"Little chilly. Not too bad."

She took my coat and I gave her the bottle of wine I'd bought on the way over, a Barolo she said was an inspired choice, because she actually preferred Italian wine to French or Californian, not that she was any kind of connoisseur, though Kyle had gone through a short-lived oenophile phase, one of the many hobbies he'd embraced and discarded over the past few years, along with fencing, electronic music, and the history of Brazil.

"Sorry," she said. "I'm babbling. I do that sometimes when I'm nervous."

"Why are you nervous?"

She made a face, like the answer was painfully obvious.

"It's just kinda weird, right? Trying to make a new friend at our age? It's like a job interview or something."

"Please don't say that," I told her. "The last thing I need right now is another job interview."

177

"See?" She smiled sadly. "I already messed up."

She brought me to the den, and we sat on the couch in front of a cozy fire. The room seemed so much bigger than it had at the party; it felt cavernous, a little desolate. The wineglass she handed me was thick stemmed, strangely heavy, with a faint, greenish tint to the glass. She saw me studying it.

"I didn't grow up like this," she said. "My dad drove a truck. I lived in a tiny house with a tiny yard. My sister and I shared a bedroom until she left for college."

"I didn't have any siblings," I told her. "It was just me and my mom."

"That must have been tough for you." She gave me a sympathetic frown. "When your mom . . ."

"It was a long time ago," I said. "But you never really get over it."

Kyle Dorfman

"So, Kyle," Buzz said. "Something interesting happened this week."

"Very interesting," Charisse confirmed. "A potential game-changer."

"Totally out of the blue," Ricky added.

"Okay," I said. "I'm listening."

Buzz looked at Ricky. Ricky looked at Charisse. Charisse looked at me.

"We need a new football coach," she said. "You would agree with that statement, wouldn't you?"

"Absolutely," I said. "One hundred percent."

They seemed relieved to hear it.

"So here's the thing," Ricky said. "I've been sniffing around, trying to see who's available, but it's just the usual suspects. I got kinda frustrated, so I called Larry Holleran to see if he had any suggestions, and you know what he said?"

I had no idea, so Charisse answered for me.

"He wants to come back." Her face broke into a delighted smile. "To Green Meadow. Can you believe that?"

"Not really," I said. "I thought he loved it out there."

"He did," Ricky replied. "But Birchfield College is in deep financial trouble. They just abolished their entire athletic program, football included. Larry's a free agent. He's ours for the taking."

"Great," I said. "Let's make it happen."

"There's one condition," Buzz told me. "And I'm not sure you're gonna like it."

Tracy Flick

We took the elevator up to the rooftop deck—yes, they had an elevator—and went straight to the sauna, a cozy cedar shack tucked between the covered patio and the hot tub.

We didn't wear bathing suits, just these thin white towels wrapped around our chests. Marissa said it was better that way, healthier and less constricting. The heat was pretty intense at first—almost lung searing—but I got used to it after a minute or two and started to breathe more easily.

When we were downstairs, I'd asked how she and Kyle had met, and she'd told me the whole saga. She was a few years out of college, living in San Francisco, trying to get a foothold in the tech world. Her best friend, Suki, started dating a coding genius named Vijay, who happened to be Kyle's college roommate. Suki introduced Marissa to Kyle, and they hit it off right away. The two couples became inseparable—they even shared a house for a while—and they got married just a few months apart. By that point Kyle and Vijay had formed the start-up that developed the *Barky* app, and it had taken off beyond their wildest projections.

"So what happened?" I asked, once we got settled in the sauna. "After they sold the company?"

"I don't want to bore you." She smoothed the towel over her stomach. "Let's talk about something else."

"It's not boring. It's like a dream come true."

"Yeah." She nodded thoughtfully. "That was what it felt like. Until it all turned to shit."

Once the money started pouring in, Vijay went a little nuts. He left Suki and their baby, moved to Hawaii with a new girlfriend, and started doing lots of drugs. The partnership dissolved, and Kyle went into business on his own, determined to prove himself to the doubters, all the people who believed that Vijay was the superstar and he was just a lucky appendage, a nobody who'd won the dorm room lottery.

"Was that true?" I asked. "About him and Vijay?"

"I don't know." She seemed pained on her husband's behalf. "It's hard to say. They were a good team, though."

"So how did Kyle manage on his own?"

The question made her smile.

"Not great," she said, as if that was an understatement. Her towel had slipped a little, so she hoisted it up and wrapped it tighter. "I should have seen it coming, Tracy. He was working all the time, and I was home with the twins—I mean, we had a nanny, but it was still pretty grueling. And then his assistant quit, and he hired a new one, this young woman fresh out of Stanford, and she was really cute, and I had a bad feeling about it, but what could I do? She was totally qualified for the job. And I'm a feminist. I'm not gonna say, *Veronika's too pretty. You're not allowed to hire her.* How does that help women?"

I nodded and a drop of sweat fell from the tip of my nose. It landed between my feet with an audible *plop*.

"It was so predictable." Marissa wiped the back of her hand across her brow. "He was traveling a lot for work, and it turned out she was going with him, and they were having a grand old time together, while I was home changing diapers. I wouldn't have even found out, except one day I stopped by Kyle's office to say hi to an old friend, and I noticed Veronika's desk was empty. I asked where she was, and my friend was like, *Oh, she's in Boston with your husband. Didn't you know?*"

"Ouch," I said. "I'm sorry."

She shrugged. It happened; they'd survived.

"I confronted him, and he admitted it right away. He broke up with her the next day and fired her a couple of weeks later. She sued the company, and it turned into a huge mess. Kyle had to step down, and we decided to change our lives, and here we are."

"What happened to Veronika?"

"Oh, she's fine, believe me. She made a lot of money from the settlement. A *lot* of money. I'm not allowed to say how much." She gave me a look, like it was just us girls up here. "I mean, I don't know about you, Tracy, but I slept with a married man in my twenties, and no one gave me one point eight million dollars."

Kyle Dorfman

I thought it was a joke at first.

"Come on," I said. "Larry Holleran doesn't want to be Principal."

"Oh yes, he does," Ricky insisted. "He got really excited when he heard that Jack was stepping down."

"It's too late," I said. "He missed the application deadline by four months."

"The timing's unfortunate," Charisse conceded. "But we can extend the search if we have to. We've done it before."

It wasn't just the timing, and they all knew it. Larry Holleran wasn't Principal material. He'd been a notoriously lazy general science teacher back in the day, famous for napping at his desk while the kids watched Jacques Cousteau. He eventually rose to the rank of Assistant Principal—the job came with a nice pay bump—but it was widely understood to be an honorary promotion, a reward for all his championships. He didn't work very hard or stay very long before ditching GMHS for Birchfield College.

"Can't he just be coach?" I asked. "Does he have to be an administrator too?"

"He needs the money," Buzz explained. "He's not doing this out of the goodness of his heart."

"Fine," I said. "Then let's just give him his old job back. Assistant Principal and Head Football Coach. That's a pretty good deal."

"We floated that," Ricky said. "But he didn't bite. He wants the big office. It's not negotiable."

"What about Tracy?" I said.

"What about her?" Buzz snapped. "She'll still be the number two. She won't be losing anything."

Tell that to Tracy, I thought.

Charisse put her hand on my arm. Her eyes were wide and hopeful.

"Marcus would be over the moon," she said. "To be able to play for Larry Holleran? That would be a dream come true."

"It'll be a new golden age," Ricky told me. "Like the nineties all over again. Remember how great that was?"

I'd played trumpet in the high school marching band, and I remembered it well, the collective euphoria of those game days, back when the football team was awesome and the whole town came out to cheer them on. I loved being in the eye of that hurricane, blowing my horn, shouting, *Hey!* and pumping my fist in the air.

"It was pretty great," I admitted.

Tracy Flick

I don't know what came over me. I could've just smiled and let the conversation flow by, the way I always did. *One point eight million dollars, what a crazy world.* Maybe it was the heat, or maybe it was the expression on Marissa's face, so open and unguarded, as if we were already friends.

"I was fifteen," I said.

"I'm sorry?" She smiled uncertainly. "You were what?"

"Fifteen." I was struck by the calmness of my own voice. I could have been telling her any random fact about myself. "The first time I slept with a married man. I was a sophomore in high school."

We stared at each other.

"Oh," she said, very softly.

"He was my English teacher," I continued, in that same matter-of-fact voice, "and I was his favorite student. I wrote a paper on *Ethan Frome*, and he gave me an A plus, the first in his entire career, at least that's what he told me. He said it was a college-level critical essay, and he wanted to know where I learned to write like that. *Like an adult,* he said. *You write like an adult.* That was how it started."

This was all true—it had happened to me—but it was hard to believe, hearing it spoken out loud like that.

"He was married." I tried to smile, for some reason, as if I were telling a funny story, but it didn't quite work. "I was fifteen."

"That's too young," she said.

"I know. But it didn't feel that way. It felt like we were equals."

"Okay." She nodded, but not the way you nod when you're agreeing with someone. "And how long did this—?"

"Not very long."

I still had that unsuccessful smile on my face, but there wasn't anything I could do about it. It was just stuck there.

"I'm sorry," she said. "I'm sorry he did that to you."

"I'm not a victim," I said. "It wasn't like that."

She got up from her bench and sat down next to me. After a moment, she put her hand on my shoulder.

"Tracy," she said. "It wasn't your fault."

"I know. But they all hated me anyway."

"No," she said. "No one hated you."

It was true, though. I'd known it at the time, but I'd done my best to forget about it, because it's not a thing you'd want to remember, being hated like that. The way people looked at me, the things they whispered as I walked down the hall.

I'm not sure what was happening on my face, but at least that stupid smile was gone.

"Oh, honey," Marissa said. "You poor thing."

I felt a weird pressure behind my eyes, like maybe I was going to cry, but it was my nose that exploded. The blood just came gushing out. I tried to catch it in my hand, but there was too much—it went right through my fingers—and you couldn't just bleed all over someone's sauna like that. I stood up and headed for the door.

"Thank you," I said, but my words were muffled by my palm. "Thank you for a lovely evening."

She told me to wait, to please not go, but I was already out of the heat and into the night, blood streaming down my face and smoke rising from my bare skin as I ran across the roof to the elevator.

PART FOUR:

Watch My Mouth

- 25 -

Kyle Dorfman was waiting in Baggage Claim, holding an iPad with Vito's name on it. He was a nerdish dude with a weirdly jacked upper body, dressed in jeans and a silky V-neck sweater. He seemed genuinely excited to shake Vito's hand.

"Welcome back, sir. We're thrilled you could join us."

"Thanks for inviting me," Vito said.

He hadn't checked any luggage, so they headed straight to the parking garage and climbed into a red Tesla that probably cost a hundred grand, though Vito couldn't say for sure. He wasn't poor, exactly, but he was no longer wealthy, and he instinctively avoided learning too much about big-ticket items he'd never be able to afford.

"Sweet ride," he said as they waited in the payment line.

"I wanted the blue one," Kyle told him. "But my wife liked the red, so . . ."

"Gotta keep the wife happy," Vito agreed, then laughed at himself. "Said the guy with three ex-wives."

Kyle made a sympathetic noise, then patted the steering wheel.

"It's a good car, though. Elon's the real deal." He glanced at Vito. "I used to know him back in the day. We weren't buddies, but you know, just to say hi at parties. We smoked a joint together once."

"Cool." Vito had known lots of famous athletes in his life, and had even met a few rock stars, including Mr. Steve Perry of Journey—a real gentleman, very down-to-earth—but he'd never crossed paths with any tech geniuses. "Maybe he'll let you ride in his rocket."

"That was another life." Kyle gave a melancholy shrug. "Now I'm President of the School Board."

"That's important too," Vito observed, and he meant it, or at least wanted to. "Education. Kids. It's a big deal."

They headed west out of the airport, zipping through the landscape of his childhood: the swamplands and toll booths, the overcrowded cemetery—the dead people of New Jersey had no room to breathe—and the faded gray water tower that meant you were almost there. Vito hadn't been back in over ten years, not since his parents left, and it seemed different somehow, cleaner and more up-to-date.

"I'm sorry your friend couldn't make it," Kyle said.

"Me too. Bad timing."

Paige had been all set to be his plus one, but a week ago she'd started working full-time as a receptionist/billing assistant for a dentist named Fred Putin (no relation to the dictator, or so he always said) who attended the same Saturday meeting they did. The job meant a lot to her—she hated being reliant on her ex for every little thing in her life—and she felt strongly that it was a bad idea to ask for three days off so soon after being hired. Vito was a little frustrated with her for not even trying, because it was a special occasion and, who knew, maybe Dr. Putin would have taken pity on her. He took out his phone and shot her a quick text.

Made it. Back in the Garden State.

On hold with Delta Dental, she replied a few seconds later.

She signed off with a kiss emoji, and he sent back two in return. Delta Dental must have picked up, because that was where it ended.

He regretted her absence even more once they arrived in Green Meadow. He wanted to show her around, give her the guided tour of his childhood haunts.

See that little house? We lived there until I was eight.

That's my elementary school. It's a senior center now.

That cul-de-sac used to be woods. I got my first blowjob in there. Ginny Huff. She was pretty cute.

There were so many sex landmarks. He could point at Debbie

Repko's house—*That's where I lost my virginity. Not in the house, though. There was a toolshed in the yard, it's probably gone now*—or take Paige to Alder Place, where the curly-haired Diamantis sisters used to live (they looked like twins, but were actually a year apart). Vito had broken up with Anastasia and immediately started up with Denise, which had caused some tension between the sisters that culminated in a fistfight on the front lawn (Anastasia won with a gut punch, but not before Denise got in a couple of good shots).

As luck would have it, the only notable house they drove past belonged to Marley Pease, a girl Vito had been with only once, at the beginning of senior year. She was totally in love with him, used to slip these handwritten notes through the vents of his locker. *You look so good in your green shirt . . . I dreamed about you last night . . . There are so many things I want to tell you . . .*

Marley wasn't as hot as most of the girls Vito had hooked up with, but they got drunk at a party one night and he didn't have any better options, so he decided to go for it. They snuck into her house and tiptoed, wasted and giggling, right past her parents' bedroom. She kept shushing him as they got undressed, but the shushes were way too loud, and Vito kept thinking they'd get caught, which made it even more exciting. He didn't bring a condom—he never did—so she used this weird spermicidal foam right before they fucked. She squatted in front of him, smiling sadly as she squirted it in—it was the only thing he remembered about having sex with her—but the foam didn't work, and she had to go to Planned Parenthood, and there weren't any sweet little notes in his locker after that.

Vito laughed out loud when he saw Kyle's house. It might have made a certain amount of sense in Beverly Hills or Coral Gables, but it looked completely bonkers on MaryBeth Way. He wasn't sure if it was modernist or postmodern or some other style he didn't know the word for, but whatever it was, it stood out like a big middle finger to the Green Meadow of his childhood, a working-class town full of affordable cookie-cutter homes. A few of those houses had been a little bigger than others; some had two-car garages or finished basements or chemically lush lawns, but everything was built on the same basic scale. There was nothing grand or swanky in the entire town, nothing that would piss off the neighbors or make them feel like losers.

"Wow," Vito said as they pulled into the driveway. "You made a statement."

Kyle looked proud and embarrassed at the same time.

"It's my wife's dream house. She was mad at me, and I gave her a blank check, and this is what happened."

"Well, I hope it cheered her up."

"A little," Kyle said. "Not as much as you'd think."

Vito was under the impression that he'd be staying in a guest room, but it turned out to be a guest *house*, a garage-sized building tucked away in a far corner of the yard. It came equipped with a queen bed, a kitchenette, and a bathroom that was a lot nicer than the one he had at home.

"There's food in the fridge," Kyle told him. "Just shoot me a text if you need anything. Otherwise we're good until the Welcome Dinner."

"The Welcome Dinner?"

"It's on your schedule." Kyle smiled a little stiffly. "You got the schedule, right?"

"Absolutely." Vito had definitely received the schedule. And he'd totally meant to look at it. "I just forgot about the dinner."

"It's not a big deal. Just you, Diane Blankenship, and the Selection Committee." He gave Vito a meaningful look. "Maybe a surprise guest or two. It'll be painless, I promise."

Vito nodded. That was all fine. But something else was bugging him.

"Can I ask you something? Who the fuck is Diane Blankenship?"

"She's the other inductee."

"I know. But who is she? What did she—"

"Front Desk Diane," Kyle said, as if that was supposed to mean something. "She's been working in the main office for almost thirty years. She was around back in our day. You don't remember?"

"Not really. I didn't pay much attention to . . ."

"Nice lady." Kyle lowered his voice. "I think the Committee just wanted some gender diversity. But you're definitely the star of the show. No question about that."

Vito shrugged. If they wanted to put the school secretary in the Hall of Fame, that was their business, though he wasn't sure why they'd picked her instead of the bus driver, or the lady who doled out the french fries.

He tried to nap, but it didn't work. He kept thinking about Marley Pease—the way she used to look at him in the hallway, that death stare of pure wounded hatred. He never said a word to her after the abortion, never checked to see how she was doing, never even acknowledged what she'd gone through. It was weird to think about the kid they didn't have, a kid who'd be a full-grown adult by now, as real to him as Jasmine or Henry.

Marley wasn't the only girl he knocked up senior year. The other one was Abbie DiScalzo, and that had been a much bigger mess. Abbie was a steady girlfriend, not a one-night stand; her family was a lot stricter and more Catholic than Vito's. There were angry phone calls, parental meetings, lots of crying and yelling and name-calling (Mr. DiScalzo kept referring to Vito as Casanova-over-Here). Abbie's asshole brother, Ray—he was a rookie cop at the time, a former linebacker for the Larks—started making threats, telling people he wanted to kick Vito's ass, or maybe break his legs, and Coach Holleran had to get involved to broker a truce between them.

The DiScalzos wanted Vito to do "the honorable thing," but he was headed to the University of Pittsburgh on a football scholarship and had no intention of saddling himself with a wife and baby. He told Abbie to do whatever she wanted—have the kid or don't have it—but to leave him the fuck out of it. In the end, she went to the clinic, just like Marley, but it broke her heart, and a lot of people took her side, including Vito's best friend, Reggie Morrison, who was number nineteen on the Apology List, the only name without a line drawn through it.

Vito and Reggie had met in sixth grade—it was their first season of Pop Warner—and they connected right away, game recognizing game, and quickly became inseparable. They were like brothers, everybody said so. They slept at each other's houses, went on vacation with each other's families, pumped iron and wrestled and got drunk in the woods, and they grew up to be the Dynamic Duo of Green Meadow, the two best football players in Lark history.

There was some rivalry between them. How could there not be? Reggie was the faster runner and better student; Vito was taller and more confident. He was also more successful with girls—he was the quarterback, after all—and Reggie couldn't help resenting him a little for that. Reggie did okay for himself—he had a sweet face and a ripped body—but he was a Black guy in an overwhelmingly white town, and he didn't have nearly as many options on that front as Vito did.

Reggie had a crush on Abbie that went all the way back to middle school. He was a little jealous when Vito started hooking up with her, but he got over it—Reggie was good that way—and the three of them spent a lot of time together. They went to the movies, the mall, the diner; sometimes they just got high and played Nintendo. It was the last semester of senior year, and they were already nostalgic for the life they'd be leaving behind.

Abbie and Reggie got to be close friends, and she started confiding in him, complaining about Vito's cheating, the mean things he said, and the fact that he forgot her birthday, even though she'd reminded him a hundred times. She liked to complain, and Vito gave her a lot to work with.

"What's wrong with you?" Reggie asked, maybe a week or two before Abbie figured out she was pregnant. "You got a great girl, why do you treat her like shit?"

"You know what?" Vito said. "You like her so much, maybe you should go out with her."

"Maybe I will," Reggie said. "Soon as she dumps your ass."

That was exactly what happened, though it took a little longer than Vito expected. Abbie and Reggie both went to Rutgers—Reggie on a football scholarship—and at some point in the spring of freshman year they became a couple. Vito didn't give a shit; he was busy with his own life. He'd had an amazing freshman season at Pitt and was already being mentioned as a possible Heisman candidate. He was training hard, partying hard, living the life. Green Meadow was a tiny dot in his rearview mirror.

He didn't go home for the summer, but Abbie and Reggie did. They tried to keep their relationship on the DL—Abbie's parents were old-school Italian American racists—but it didn't work, because you couldn't keep something like that quiet in Green Meadow.

The way Vito heard it, Reggie came out of the gym one night and found Ray DiScalzo waiting by his car. Ray was a cop, but he wasn't on duty. He just wanted to deliver a private message, a friendly request for Reggie to stay the fuck away from his little sister. Reggie asked why, and Ray said, *You know why*, and Reggie said, *Be a man, say it to my face*, and it went on like that until Ray said the word, and Reggie beat the shit out of him in the parking lot, just left him lying there, moaning on the pavement.

Reggie was charged with felony assault, and things looked bad for him, a Black athlete who'd put a white cop in the hospital (the fight had left Ray with a concussion and a broken jaw). Reggie's mom was beside herself. She called Vito and begged him to write a letter on behalf of her son, a character reference, so the Judge would know that Reggie was an upstanding citizen, a good friend and teammate, and a person who would never resort to violence unless he was provoked.

"No problem," he told her. "I'll get right on it."

He fully intended to write the letter. Why wouldn't he? He hated Ray DiScalzo and didn't want Reggie to go to jail. Sure, they'd drifted apart a little, but deep down they were brothers, and he knew Reggie would do the same for him if the situation were reversed.

It was such a simple favor—it would have taken a half hour of his time at the most—but he never did it, not even after Mrs. Morrison called him two more times. In the end, it didn't matter. Coach Holleran was friends with the County Prosecutor, and he made a call or two, and the charges were eventually dropped. It took some time, though; Reggie missed his entire sophomore season, and he just gave up—never played football again, never finished college. The last Vito heard, Reggie had joined the Army, and after that it was like he'd dropped off the face of the earth.

It had been a long time since Vito had walked the streets of Green Meadow. The houses were pale and modest and pressed too close together. Lawn, driveway, lawn, driveway, lawn, as far as the eye could see, and nobody on the sidewalk except for him, like he had the whole town to himself.

The Morrisons lived on Logan Street, south of the railroad tracks, near the plastics factory. Precision Extrusion was gone now—an expensive-looking condo complex had taken its place—and the neighborhood felt busier and more prosperous than it used to. Reggie's old house was unchanged, though—beige vinyl siding, brick front steps, tarnished brass mailbox—so Vito was more surprised than he should have been when a white woman in her late thirties answered the door. She was wearing workout clothes, breathing hard, holding a TV remote in her hand.

"Can I help you?" She was shifting her weight from foot to foot, trying to keep her heart rate up.

"I'm not sure," he said. "It's just . . . I used to know the people who lived here."

She stopped moving her feet. "The Morrisons?"

"Yeah. Do you know them?"

"Not really. I met Mrs. Morrison once, but . . . you know, we didn't talk that much. She seemed like a nice lady."

"You wouldn't know how to get in touch with her, would you?"

She pursed her lips, sorry to disappoint him.

"I think she moved into an assisted living place, but I'm not sure which one. And that was four years ago, so . . ." The woman smiled sadly, not wanting to complete the thought. "Maybe some of the older neighbors would know."

"I'm trying to find her son," Vito explained. "He was my friend growing up. Great football player. Really good guy."

"I'm sure he was." The woman nodded vaguely. This was more information than she needed. "I really have to—"

"I owe him an apology," Vito said. "I'm in a twelve-step program, I'm trying to make amends to people I hurt."

"Well, good luck with that." She backed away from the threshold. "You have a nice day."

The door closed politely in his face.

Vito stood there for a few seconds with his mouth hanging open. He felt a weird urge to ring the bell again, like maybe this time the universe would realign and Reggie's mom would appear, or maybe even Reggie himself, so he could say what needed to be said and get this weight off his chest, but it wasn't gonna happen—not today, maybe not ever.

Before starting back to Kyle's, he took a picture of Reggie's house and texted it to Paige.

My best friend used to live here.

I miss you.

He felt a little queasy as he slipped the phone back into his pocket, but he shook it off and started down the street towards the condos. It was chillier now, and a light rain had begun to fall.

He stopped and studied the new building. Some of the condo units were gray and some were yellow, and they all had balconies. The sign out front read *Meadow Branch Commons: A Unique Experience in Residential Luxury.* The words made no sense. Something buzzed in his pocket. He had a question, at least it felt like a question, but he didn't know what it was, and then it was gone, and there was nothing in his head but radio static, and then that was gone too, and his mind was a blank.

- 26 -

Nate Cleary

Kelly was up in her room, all set to go. The blackout shades were down, the ring light was glowing, the webcam was mounted on its tripod. I handed her the cookie tin without breaking into frame.

"Is this for me?" Her voice was a startled whisper. "You're so sweet. What did you bring me?"

She took her time undoing the ribbon, making a project out of it. She was really good at stuff like that. Unscrewing. Untying. Uncapping.

"Something smells really good, *Tap Tap Tap.*"

She pried off the lid, slowly and cautiously, as if there might be a bomb inside. She waited a moment, letting the camera linger on the cookies inside.

"Mmmm. White chocolate chips, red M&M's, and walnuts. You know me so well." She made a sad but sexy face. "I'll have to save them for later. I put on some special lipstick just for you, and I don't want to mess it up. Is that okay?"

I nodded yes. That was my whole job. To stand behind the webcam so she could look at me while she talked. She said it helped to keep her focused.

"I'm so lucky to have you in my life," she whispered. "You knew I was feeling a little down, and you baked my favorite cookies for me. From scratch, *Tap Tap Tap.* You're so thoughtful and caring."

And then she did the thing I loved, licking her lips in slow motion, all the way around, just the pointy tip of her tongue. It was a thrill to watch her do it in real time, knowing that thousands of people would watch it later on YouTube.

"You're the best boyfriend ever."

It never failed, the way her voice went straight into my blood-stream, like a drug. She knew it too. Sometimes, when we were hooking up, she'd whisper *Tap Tap Tap* into my ear, and it always sent me right over the edge.

It was raining when I left her house. Not hard, just a misty drizzle. I got into my car and sat there for a few seconds. I had that feeling you get when you go to a movie in the afternoon, and the world seems unreal when you come out. It was always that way after I helped Kelly with a video.

It was nice, being told over and over again what a great boyfriend I was. But it was also a little weird, because I wasn't really that great. I was just following instructions. She told me what cookies to bake and how to wrap them, and that's what I did.

But that was okay. I liked making her happy, and I liked being part of her work. It felt grown-up in a way that none of my other relationships ever had.

I liked her so much that it made me a little sad about graduating and heading off to college. I still didn't know where I was going, but there was a decent chance that I'd end up at Hamilton or Washing-ton University or Davidson, and that would be the end of me and Kelly. I tried to talk to her about it a couple of times, but she just shrugged it off, like September was a million years away, and there was no point worrying about it. It made me wonder if she'd even miss me when I was gone.

I was so deep in thought, I drove right past him. He was just part of the scenery, a tall man sitting on the curb in front of the new condos, looking dejected, getting rained on. I was halfway down the block before something clicked in my brain—*Holy shit, I know that guy!*— and I hung a quick U-turn and drove back to where he was sitting.

I asked if he was okay, and he gave me this blank look, like he wasn't really sure, and then I asked if he was Vito Falcone, and he seemed surprised for a second, like he hadn't expected to be recognized, even though he was the most famous person who'd ever lived in our town.

"That's right," he said, and he sounded almost relieved. "I'm Vito Falcone."

- 27 -

Tracy Flick

I didn't want to go to the Welcome Dinner. I didn't want to meet the star quarterback, or share a meal with my colleagues on the Selection Committee. I just wanted to be left alone.

You think it'll make you feel better, telling your secret to someone, getting that poison out of your system, but it didn't work like that for me. It just unlocked a lot of bad memories, and questions I didn't know how to answer.

I had this image in my head, Mr. Dexter and me in the darkroom after school. I had my hand in his pants and he was giving me instructions: *Faster now, but loosen up a little.* It didn't seem real—I thought maybe I was making it up—except that I remembered all these yearbook photos drying on the line, the happy faces of kids who weren't my friends—they were making wire sculptures in art class, giving each other piggyback rides, playing racquetball in gym class, normal things like that.

There you go, he told me. *That's more like it.*

Who was the girl who did that? I didn't recognize her. And how had my mother let it happen? That was the part I kept tripping over. I couldn't help thinking that she was at fault somehow—that she should have known—because the two of us were so close, we were best friends, we were like one person. But maybe it wasn't really like that? Maybe we just said those things to make ourselves feel better?

Where were you? I wondered. *Why didn't you stop me?*

But I didn't want to be mad at my mother—she'd had such a hard life—so I blamed Marissa instead, even though I knew on some level that she didn't deserve it. All she'd done was reach out and try to be my friend, and it had worked, probably a lot better than either of us had expected. I lowered my guard and told her who I was, and I'd lost control of myself in the process. I resented her for that, for allowing me to be so vulnerable.

We hadn't talked since that night in the sauna. She'd called me a few times—more than a few, actually—asking if I was okay, giving me the name of a therapist she knew. She also left a series of small gifts on my front stoop—flowers, a bag of loose tea, a bath bomb— always accompanied by a brief note on that handmade paper, saying she was thinking of me, inviting me to go for a walk or meet her for coffee, whatever I wanted. She also delivered the humidifier, which I'd forgotten about in the chaos of my departure, despite her many reminders. The ironic thing was, I didn't need it anymore, because the nosebleeds had stopped, as abruptly and mysteriously as they'd started.

That was the only good news in my life. On every other front, it felt like I was unraveling, failing as a mother, as an administrator, as a functional human being. Daniel and Margaret knew I was depressed, and they were picking up the slack with Sophia, who'd been staying with them for the past couple of weeks. I felt guilty about that, but it was a lifesaver to come home to an empty house and just be able to collapse, not have to worry about meals or homework or trying to be a good parent.

I didn't have anything to spare. I woke up tired in the morning, and the feeling never lifted. It was all I could do to drag my body to the places it was required to go, because I was stubborn and didn't want to admit defeat.

So of course I went to the Welcome Dinner. I didn't have a choice. I got dressed, trudged out to my car, and drove to the Terminal, the railroad-themed restaurant they'd built in the old Green Meadow train station. And then I summoned everything I had and walked into that banquet room, standing tall and smiling brightly, because I was a leader and needed to act like one.

Kyle Dorfman

Tracy was a few minutes late to the dinner. Marissa had been worried about her—she wouldn't tell me why—and had asked me to check on her well-being. But Tracy seemed fine to me, standing in the doorway with her usual ramrod posture and that chipper smile on her face. I waved her over and introduced her to Vito.

"Vito, this is Dr. Flick, our Assistant Principal. Tracy, this is Vito Falcone, our guest of honor."

Vito stood up—he was wearing a silver blazer and an open-collared shirt—and offered his big hand to Tracy. He was bulkier than he'd been in high school, but less imposing somehow—gray at the temples, a little anxious around the eyes.

"Hello, Doctor."

"One of our two guests of honor," Tracy corrected me. She nodded at Front Desk Diane, who was sitting in the middle of the long table, next to Charisse Turner, across from Jack Weede and Ricky Pizzoli.

"Of course," I said. "Props to Diane as well."

Tracy had to crane her neck to meet Vito's gaze.

"Thanks so much for joining us," she said. "You're such a role model to our students."

"Tell that to my kids." Vito smiled sadly. "They're not too impressed with their dad these days."

"That's the way it goes," I told him. "No man's a hero in his own house."

There was an empty seat next to Buzz, and Tracy figured it was hers. She started to pull out the chair, but I stopped her.

"That one's reserved," I said. "You're over here."

I took her gently by the arm and escorted her to the far end of the table, where Nate and Lily were sitting, along with Lily's plus one.

"I didn't realize there was a seating chart," Tracy muttered.

"There's not," I said. "It's just, Vito has a friend coming, so . . ."

She shrugged, like it was all the same to her. Then she smiled gamely and sat down with the kids.

Jack Weede

Diane looked up from her menu.

"Alice didn't feel like coming?"

"She's away for the week. Visiting her brother in Vermont."

"Oh." She reached for the wine bottle. "Good for her."

She filled her own glass, then offered some to me.

"Not too much," I said. "Some of us have to work in the morning."

Diane didn't have to worry about that. She was taking the day off to prepare for the Induction Ceremony, getting a deluxe spa treatment with her sister—massage, mani-pedi, blowout, facial—the whole nine yards.

"You could always call in sick," she suggested. "I won't tell the boss."

"That's not a bad idea," I said. "Maybe I'll join you at the spa."

She nodded, as if she was open to that possibility.

"I'm sure you could use a pedicure. No offense, Jack, but your toes were never your best feature."

I glanced around to see if anyone was eavesdropping, but our neighbors were busy with their own conversations. We were an island unto ourselves.

"I bet yours are still cute, though." I lowered my voice. "Prettiest ones I ever saw."

We'd had a whole foot thing for a while. She'd come to school in open-toed shoes every Friday, her toenails painted whatever color I'd requested. I got down on my knees and sucked on them a few times—I enjoyed the earthy, slightly funky taste—but it just made her giggle.

"You should put that in your speech," she said.

"I did," I told her. "It's the whole second paragraph."

Lily Chu

It was actually kind of fun at the restaurant. Clem and I were holding hands and eating off each other's plates, and it wasn't as big a deal as I thought it would be. Nate was surprised at first, but he was cool about it, and the adults pretended not to notice.

It was such a relief, after all the playacting at my house. We were being super cautious around my parents, making it very clear that we were just *friends-from-camp*, sleeping in separate rooms, keeping some space between us when we sat on the couch. Even so, I could tell my mother was worried—my father was clueless, as usual—probably just from the way Clem kept looking at me, like I was the best movie ever, and they didn't want to miss a second of it.

Kyle Dorfman

Vito had been fine when I picked him up at the airport, and he was still in a good mood when I'd left him in the guest house. Something must have happened after that, though, because he seemed moody and distracted in the restaurant, almost to the point of being rude.

"Who's better?" Ricky asked him. "Brady or Manning? In your personal opinion."

Vito grimaced, like the question caused him pain.

"I'm talking about Peyton," Ricky said, in case there'd been some confusion. "Not Eli. I mean, that goes without saying, but—"

"Brady." Vito spoke the name through gritted teeth, then reached up and tugged on his earlobe, really hard, almost like he was trying to yank it off his head. "Oh, fuck."

"You okay?" I asked.

"Just a headache," he muttered. "I get them sometimes."

"You need a Tylenol?"

"I already took some. They don't always work."

"Is it a migraine?" Charisse asked.

"Nope." Vito winced again. "I just played a little too much football."

He pressed his fingers to his temples, like a psychic communing with the dead. I was about to ask him if he wanted to go back to the guest house and lie down, but I didn't get a chance, because right then, Larry Holleran burst into the room with his arms spread wide, like he wanted to embrace the world.

"Hot damn," he said. "You are a bunch of good-looking people!"

Tracy Flick

I'd had a bad feeling the minute I walked into that room. Kyle was nervous and wouldn't meet my eyes. Buzz looked even more smug than he had at our interview. I didn't understand why Charisse Turner and Ricky Pizzoli were even there—they had nothing to do with the Hall of Fame—and I couldn't ask anyone, because I'd been exiled to the Siberian end of the table, as far from the action as I could get.

But now I knew. For a second or two I was almost relieved, the way you are when you forget a name and then it comes back to you.

Larry Holleran.

You should have seen the way they greeted him—*Coach! Great to see you! Welcome home!*—their voices full of joy and wonder, like he'd returned from the dead.

So that's who it is.

The job search had been stalled for weeks, and I hadn't been able to figure out why. I'd heard a rumor that a new candidate had popped up at the last minute, but that was it. No name, no identifying details. Just a rumor.

It hadn't made sense at the time. I knew my competition—it's a small world in secondary ed—and all my rivals were out of the running, including Angela Vargas, the only one who'd seemed like a genuine threat. I asked Jack if he'd heard anything and he said no, and told me to relax, because these things always take longer than you think they will. I'd thought about calling Kyle again, but I didn't want to look too needy or paranoid. I figured he would warn me if something bad was happening, and maybe give me some advice about how to deal with it, because we were friends, and he was on my side.

But that was my mistake, because Kyle wasn't my friend and the knife was already in my back.

- 28 -

Jack Weede

I walked Diane out to her car. She'd had several glasses of wine over the course of dinner.

"You sure you're okay to drive? I'm happy to take you home if—"

"Thank you," she said. "But I'm fine."

The night was windy and clear. She was wearing a dark coat I'd never seen before. It had a nubbly texture and gave her a flattering youthful silhouette. I was a slouching old man in a rumpled sport coat.

"That was nice," I said. "I'm glad we got a chance to catch up a little. It's been a long time."

"It has." She glanced back at the restaurant. Some members of our group were loitering near the entrance, talking and laughing, not wanting the night to end. "I can't believe Larry Holleran showed up. He hasn't changed a bit."

"I bet he dyes his hair," I said. "You can't be that age and not have a little gray, right?"

Larry had always been vain. He used to brag about doing a hundred push-ups and a hundred sit-ups first thing every morning, and would challenge his football players to punch him in the stomach as hard as they could.

Go ahead, he'd tell them. *You can't hurt me.*

But they would never do it. They were too afraid.

"Is he moving back here?" She had to hold her hair down to keep it from blowing in her face. "It kinda sounded like he was."

I'd noticed that too. Larry had made a toast during dessert. He said how great it was to see us all again, and joked that we might be seeing a lot more of him in the future.

"I hope not," I said. "I like him a lot better when he's in Pennsylvania."

"What do you care?" She was smiling, but there was an edge in her voice. "You're gonna be out in your RV, living the dream. You're gonna forget all about us."

"I won't forget you," I said.

Our dinner companions had finished their goodbyes, and now they were heading in our direction, pressing their key fobs, their cars blinking and chirping in response.

"Oh, Jack." She stepped forward and hugged me, the first time we'd embraced in almost a decade. Her coat felt rough against my hand, but only for a second, and then she stepped back, out of my reach. "You take care of yourself, okay?"

"You too," I said. "I'll see you tomorrow."

Tracy Flick

I made it through the rest of dinner on autopilot, keeping one eye on Larry Holleran and the other on Kyle, my ears tuned to the conversation on the other side of the room. I tried to slow down, to convince myself that I was jumping to a bad conclusion, but the wet cement in my stomach told me otherwise. I'd been betrayed before; I knew what it felt like.

And Larry wasn't even trying to hide it. He made a circuit of the table, shaking hands like a politician working the rope line, looking everyone in the eye, radiating authority and easy masculine charm, the self-confidence of a proven winner. He grabbed my hand in both of his and squeezed a little too hard.

"Tracy, honey. It's good to see you again. I've been hearing great things about your work. I'm gonna need to pick your brain a little one of these days. Get to know you a little better."

"Please don't call me *honey*," I told him.

"Yes, ma'am." He nodded crisply, as if I were his superior officer. "Your preferences are duly noted."

I wanted to confront Kyle, but I didn't trust myself, not with the other Board members around, so I fled the restaurant as soon as I could, before the fake smile melted off my face, and drove straight home. I pulled into my driveway, sat there for a few seconds, and pulled right back out again.

You've got to do something. You can't just let this happen.

I went to the Lemon Drop Tavern, ordered a Manhattan at the bar, and tried to think.

What's going on? I texted Kyle. *Is there something you need to tell me?*

Five minutes went by. No answer.

I thought you were my friend.

Two more minutes.

LARRY HOLLERAN??? ARE YOU FUCKING KIDDING ME!!!

Larry may have been an excellent football coach, but he was a terrible Assistant Principal. I knew this firsthand, because I'd had to clean up his mess. He botched the schedule, made terrible hiring decisions, and was wildly inconsistent on disciplinary matters. His evaluations and reports were unreadable, completely useless, because he didn't know what he was talking about and wasn't smart enough to fake it.

This is amazing, Jack used to tell me when I first came on board. *I can actually understand what you write.*

But I also knew that it didn't matter. Larry Holleran was a local legend, a charming loudmouth, the man who brought home the trophies.

And who was I? I was nobody. A woman. A lowly bureaucrat. A doctor in quotation marks. It didn't matter that I was better than he was—smarter and more competent and harder working and more dedicated to the kids.

I couldn't win.

They wouldn't let me.

Kyle Dorfman

We had an after-party at my house, a casual rooftop gathering. There were six of us seated around the teak fire table, the blue flames flickering up through a bed of smooth gray river stones.

"I can't wait to work with your son," Larry Holleran told Charisse. "I've been hearing great things about him."

To be honest, I was a little annoyed with Larry. We'd asked him to play it cool at the restaurant—it was a delicate situation with the job search, and there were still some procedural wrinkles to iron out—but he just walked in and dominated the room, acting like the job was already his. He was sending us a not-so-subtle signal, letting us know that he'd be calling his own shots from now on, and wouldn't be interested in a lot of guidance or oversight. My colleagues didn't seem to mind, though.

"Marcus is amazing," Ricky said. "He can run and he can throw and he can see the whole field. He's the real deal."

Charisse smiled proudly. "He's been recruited by so many private schools. Full scholarships, all kinds of perks. But he wants to stay right here in Green Meadow."

"He's a great student," Buzz added. "A real scholar-athlete."

Larry nodded judiciously. "Well, I'll see what I can do with him. I'm sure he's got some bad habits he needs to unlearn." He yanked his thumb at Vito. "I know this one did. He showed up freshman year, thinking he was hot shit, that he had nothing to learn from anyone. But I disabused him of that notion pretty quickly, didn't I, Vito?"

Vito didn't answer. He was hunched over on the couch, elbows on his knees, staring into the fire.

"Didn't I?" Larry repeated, a little louder.

Vito blinked a few times, like he was waking from a trance.

"Sorry," he said. "Can you repeat the question?"

Tracy Flick

Kyle wasn't answering his phone, so I drove to his house. And then I got there and saw all those cars and the lights on the roof and heard the voices wafting down. It hurt to be excluded like that. Schemed against. Disrespected.

It wasn't right.

Marissa was surprised to see me at the door.

"Tracy." Her face was full of concern. "Are you okay?"

"I'm here for the party," I told her.

She said something else, but I was already past her, on my way up to the roof.

Kyle Dorfman

She came charging out of the elevator, fists clenched, leading with her chin.

"What's going on here?" she demanded. "What's this all about?"

"Whoa, Tracy." I stood up, raised my hands in a calming gesture. "Take it easy."

She stopped near the Ping-Pong table. She was breathing hard through her nose, almost vibrating with rage.

"Do you think I'm a piece of garbage?" she asked. "You think you can just crumple me up and toss me in a trash can? Is that what you think?"

"What? No. What are you talking about?"

She smiled in a way that worried me.

"You're a liar, Kyle. A liar and a cheater and a backstabber."

"Dr. Flick." Buzz's voice was clipped and cautionary. "If I were you, I'd watch my mouth."

"Watch my mouth?" she snapped. "*Watch my mouth?* Who the fuck do you think you are?"

Buzz was shocked. We all were.

"I'm the Superintendent of Schools," he replied. "I'm your boss, in case you forgot, or maybe you're too drunk to care."

"I'm not drunk," she said, though she didn't sound a hundred percent sober, either. "I see what you're doing here. And I won't allow it."

"What?" I said. "What does that even mean?"

She stared at me for a long moment, clenching and unclenching her fists.

"You heard me," she said. "I won't allow it."

And then she turned and stormed back to the elevator.

Tracy Flick

It was so lame, something a child would say.

I won't allow it.

The truth was the opposite, of course.

They would do whatever they wanted. And they would crush me, the way they always did.

I wasn't crying when I got downstairs, but I was close. Marissa was waiting for me, that look of pity unchanged on her face. She reached for my arm, but I swatted it away.

I rushed out the door, hurrying down the curving path to the driveway. I stopped and stared at Kyle's Tesla—even in the dark it was glossy and obscenely red—and I couldn't help thinking how good it would feel to take a baseball bat to the windshield, to watch it dissolve in a cascade of sparkling shards, how good it would feel, just once in my life, to be the perpetrator, the one who did the damage.

But I didn't have a baseball bat, so I just kicked the driver's side door as hard as I could. To my astonishment, the metal gave way beneath my foot—you could hear it crumple—leaving a small but very conspicuous dent in the shiny surface. I was all set to do it again, but the alarm went off, and it was really loud—almost deafening—so I decided to leave well enough alone.

222

- 29 -

Jack Weede

I had trouble getting to sleep, but that wasn't unusual. It had been that way ever since my heart attack. I think some part of me was always scared that I wasn't going to wake up in the morning.

I watched an episode of *Seinfeld* and a bit of Jimmy Fallon, an interview with a Scandinavian actress I'd never heard of. They just kept coming, these young people, wave after wave of them, beautiful and full of energy, hungry for the world. It gets to be too much after a while.

I must have dozed off on the couch because that was where I woke up. I was aware of a faint clicking sound, and then another one, and another after that. I got up and opened the front door.

Diane was standing on my lawn, gazing up at my bedroom window on the second floor. She was wearing the same coat as before, but she had a nightgown under it instead of a dress.

"What are you doing?" I asked.

"What does it look like?" She leaned back and tossed another pebble. "I'm trying to wake you up."

PART FIVE:

Dead Woman Walking

- 30 -

Glenn thought it would be a bigger deal. You hear about a "red car-pet" and you can't help thinking fancy hotels, gowns and tuxes, a hundred flashbulbs popping at the same time. But it was just the side entrance of Green Meadow High School on a drab March evening, the doors you would use if you took the bus, not even the main entrance with the portico.

They did have a carpet; it was more maroon than red, maybe thirty feet long, shimmery and slightly wrinkled, a little narrower than the sidewalk it covered. A velvet rope ran along one side, and Glenn was standing on a patch of grass behind the barrier, along with a small crowd of fans and well-wishers. Some of them were there for Vito—a couple of guys in Dolphins jerseys with FALCONE written across the back, and three middle-aged women in cheer-leader outfits, not bad-looking, actually, though their cartwheel days were over—but there were also a fair number of high school stu-dents wearing T-shirts and holding signs that read TEAM DIANE, in honor of the school secretary. Glenn remembered her fondly from his student days; she was young and pretty back then, barely out of high school herself, and she'd always smiled and waved when she saw him. He was flattered for a while, until he realized that she smiled and waved at everyone. That was her thing—being nice to the whole world—and she'd ridden that horse all the way into the Hall of Fame.

Good for her, he thought. *At least she's a decent person.*

There was a woman cop on duty, wandering in and out of the

227

school building, checking out the spectators, making sure everyone was behaving themselves and staying off the red carpet. She was short and thickly built, almost egg-shaped in her protective vest, her reddish hair tucked up under her hat. She was probably the School Resource Officer, because she seemed to know a lot of the kids by name, and was comfortable joking around with them.

She was saying something into her shoulder radio—Glenn couldn't quite make out the words—when one of the cheerleader ladies tapped him on the back.

"Excuse me?" She nodded at the yearbook in Glenn's hand. "Were you Class of '94?"

Holy shit, Glenn thought. *It's Ginny Huff.*

Ginny had been one of the hottest seniors when Glenn was a freshman; the guys in his class talked about her like she was a goddess. Now she was just a mom playing dress-up.

"I was '97," Glenn told her. "This is my brother's yearbook."

"Oh," she said. "Who's your brother?"

"I don't think you knew him."

"Try me." She smiled proudly. "I was on the yearbook staff. I knew everyone."

"His name was Carl. Carl Keeler."

"Oh." Ginny's smile faded. "I remember Carl."

I bet you did, Glenn wanted to tell her. *And I bet you thought it was hilarious when Vito humiliated him in front of the whole school.*

He didn't get a chance to say it, though, because Ginny's attention had already shifted, along with everyone else's, to the Town Car that had just pulled up to the curb. Glenn felt a surge of adrenaline move through his body as the chauffeur got out and opened the back door, but it turned out to be a false alarm. The man who emerged was old and a little stooped, and it took Glenn a second or two to recognize him as Jack Weede.

There was a smattering of polite applause as the Principal made his way down the red carpet. One of the kids threw a handful of confetti at his head, a little harder than necessary. Weede stopped and stared into the crowd, looking a little annoyed as he brushed himself off.

"You might want to save that for the important people," he said.

* * *

It reminded Diane of her wedding day, and not in a good way. She was tired and cranky—sandwiched between her father and sister in the back seat of the limo—and her dress was a little too tight. And of course her sister wouldn't shut up, because silence was her sworn enemy.

"We're going to the high school, Daddy. You remember the high school, right?" Gail leaned forward so she could see their father's face. "You went there a long time ago. Diane works there now."

Their father gave a vague nod, like all that was fine with him. Diane hoped he would stay like this, sweet and placid, but you never knew. He could get disoriented sometimes, and even a little belligerent, which was why they hardly ever took him anywhere. But Diane wanted him at the ceremony. What was the point of getting inducted into the Hall of Fame if your loved ones couldn't be there to watch? And besides, she thought, maybe some tiny part of him was still awake in there. Maybe he'd be proud of her, even if he couldn't say so.

"You met Mommy in high school," Gail reminded him. "Her name was Marie Coluccio. You remember Marie, don't you?"

"Marie's right here," their father said. He placed his hand on Diane's knee and gave it a squeeze. "She's my girl."

"No, Daddy," Gail said. "That's Diane. She's your daughter. Marie's not with us anymore. Remember what a pretty singing voice she had?"

Oh God, Diane thought. *Not this.*

Gail hummed a few bars, and then she started singing, very softly. Her voice wasn't nearly as good as their mother's.

"Almost heaven, West Virginia. Blue Ridge Mountains, Shen—"

"Please." Diane slit her throat with her index finger. "I can't with the singing. Not right now."

Gail was offended, but she stopped.

"Are you okay?"

"I'm just tired." Diane removed her father's hand from her leg. "I didn't sleep well."

She left it at that, because there was no point explaining that the reason she was tired was that she'd spent the night with Jack inside his giant RV. Gail had always disapproved of their relationship—of course she had; what was there to approve of?—and she'd been frustrated by Diane's failure to get over it and move on with her life. Diane didn't blame her for that. She was frustrated too.

It had been wonderful, though, being alone with Jack again. They hadn't had sex, hadn't even tried. They just talked for a while, and then they held each other—he felt so frail and bony in her arms—and then they fell asleep together on the fold-down bed, which was surprisingly roomy and comfortable. It was the first night they'd ever spent together, and there wouldn't be another, but that was okay. It felt like an ending—a proper goodbye—the closure that had been denied her for all those years. It was going to be awkward, though, seeing him again at the ceremony, listening to him make a speech that would undoubtedly be witty and touching, but would omit the essential truth, which was that they'd loved each other for a while, and then he'd broken her heart. But it was better than nothing, she supposed, better than being ignored and forgotten.

This is my life, she thought as they turned onto the access road that led to the high school. *It's the only one I have.*

There were a lot of people waiting by the side entrance, and they cheered when she got out of the limo.

"It's Diane!"

"Front Desk Diane!"

"Looking good, Diane!"

Gail went first, hustling across the red carpet, covering her face with her hands as if she'd just been arrested for a terrible crime, and then it was Diane's turn. She threaded her arm through her father's, just as she had on her wedding day, and they started walking towards the school. It was slow going—her father took tiny, shuffling steps—but that was fine with Diane. She wanted to savor every second. She remembered how unhappy her father had been walking her to the altar, because he disliked Lance and thought she was making a mistake, and of course he'd been right. He was happier now, just a little puzzled by the applause and the confetti.

"Is this for me?" he whispered.

"It's for both of us," she said, and pulled him a little closer.

* * *

Paige called while Vito was on his way to the high school. He thought about sending her to voicemail, but he'd been avoiding her all day and felt guilty about it.

"Hey," he said. "I can't talk for long. I'm five minutes from the red carpet."

"You're so fancy," she said. "I just ate a microwave burrito in my sweatpants."

"I'm jealous," Vito told her, and he meant it. He would've been a lot happier sitting with Paige at her little round table, peeling an orange they could share for dessert. "How was your day?"

"I got through it. How's it going up there?"

"Not bad," he said. "Uneventful."

He hated lying to her. The trip had been way too eventful already, and he still had to get through the fucking ceremony. He wanted to tell Paige about what had happened yesterday—the blackout he'd suffered after going to Reggie's house—but it would have to wait until he got home, because it wasn't the kind of bomb you could drop on someone over the phone. He was dreading it, though, because he knew it would scare her, and she had enough problems in her life already.

"I wish I was there," she told him. "I bet you look really handsome in your suit."

"I'm actually wearing my high school game jersey. A replica anyway. It's a gift from the rich guy."

231

"You should bring it home." Her voice was softer now, a little sultry. "I'll wear it to bed if you want me to."

This was not the first time a woman had made this offer to Vito. He didn't understand the appeal, didn't have the slightest interest in fucking anyone in a football jersey, not even Paige, but he figured that could wait for later too.

"Whatever you want," he said. They were at the high school. He could see a crowd gathered by the side entrance. "I'll see you tomorrow."

"I can't wait," she told him. "Take a selfie for me, okay? I want to see what you look like in your uniform."

*   *   *

It got dark while Glenn waited. One limo after another pulled up to the red carpet—actually, there were only two Town Cars, they just made multiple trips—but it was always somebody else who stepped out. The bald Superintendent. The *Barky* guy and his family. The Assistant Principal, who looked a little manic. A couple of high school kids. Front Desk Diane, who must have been close to fifty now, and her father, who looked a little out of it.

But then another limo arrived, and this time it was Vito, wearing his old football jersey, number twelve, and everybody started going crazy, calling out his name and telling him they loved him, and the asshole didn't even have the courtesy to wave hello, because he was too busy taking a fucking selfie, gazing up at his phone with his most soulful and manly expression.

He took several photos from slightly different angles, and when he was finally satisfied, he put his phone away and started walking down the carpet, moving with the easy glide of an athlete, nodding and smiling at the crowd.

Glenn's heart was pounding in his ears, so loud that he almost forgot his plan, which was to confront Vito and show him Carl's picture in the yearbook.

Remember him? Glenn was going to say. *I want you to look at his face.*

That was the first thing he needed to do, and he almost did it. He pushed right up to the velvet rope and called Vito's name, and Vito turned and looked right at him, a quizzical half smile on his face, like he was wondering if they knew each other. But before Glenn could call him over, he was jostled from behind, hard enough that he dropped the yearbook. It was the cheerleader ladies who did it, shoving past him as they ducked under the rope, giggling at their own audacity.

They surrounded Vito and greeted him with a cheer, shaking their pom-poms and spelling out the letters of his name—*Give me a V*, all that stupid bullshit—and then they pranced around him in their little skirts and saddle shoes as he walked into the building. The lady cop didn't seem to mind; she just grinned, as if the cheerleaders had every right to ignore the barrier that everyone else had to respect, and Glenn didn't do anything, either. He just stood there dumbstruck, like a useless freshman in the cafeteria, too weak and scared to stand up for his own brother.

- 31 -

Tracy Flick

I wore a black cocktail dress to the ceremony, along with sheer black stockings, and black shoes with high heels. The dress was short and sleeveless, and I looked good in it, if I may say so myself.

"Dr. Flick." Buzz gave me a tight fake smile as I entered the Green Room, which was really just the Band Room. "Nice to see you."

"Big crowd out there," Kyle said. "Really good energy."

I wasn't fooled by their politeness. I was a dead woman walking and we all knew it. You couldn't curse out the Superintendent and call the Board President a lying backstabber and expect to keep your job, not that I even wanted to. I had no interest in being Larry Holleran's little helper. Someone else was going to have to clean up his mess this time.

I said hello to Lily and Nate—they were all dressed up for the occasion, cheerfully oblivious to the adult intrigue—and waved to Jack, who gave me a subtle nod of commiseration. He'd taken the day off, so we hadn't been able to talk in person, but he'd texted me in the afternoon, after speaking to Buzz. He wanted me to know how upset he was on my behalf, and to assure me that he hadn't been in on the conspiracy. *It's crazy,* he wrote. *You're twice as good as Larry and they know it.* I appreciated his support, not that it made any difference. Jack was a lame duck, no longer a factor in anyone's calculations, and now I was one too.

I sat down on a piano bench and pretended to review my notes, wondering why I'd even bothered to show up. It would have served them right if I'd stayed home, left them in the lurch at the last minute, but I was too proud and stubborn for that. I said I'd be there, and I always kept my word, so there I was. I would get up on that stage, and I would be the smiling Master of Ceremonies, and I would perform that task the same way I'd performed a thousand other important tasks during my tenure at GMHS, with quiet competence and unstinting professionalism, and I wouldn't let my personal feelings get in the way. I owed that to myself, not to anyone else.

When Vito Falcone and Front Desk Diane finally arrived, we took a group photo, all eight of us with our arms around one another. I was standing on the far left, next to Jack. When it was over, he gave me a fatherly squeeze on the shoulder.

"You okay?" he whispered.

"Fine," I said. "Never better."

A few minutes before showtime, we walked as a group from the Green Room to the auditorium. I lagged behind, keeping out of the fray, but Kyle detached himself from the pack, and waited for me by the backstage door, arms folded indignantly across his chest.

"What did you do to my car?" he asked.

"I have no idea what you're talking about." I held his gaze for a moment or two. "But sometimes people reap what they sow."

"Goddammit, Tracy." He stared at me in wounded disbelief, as if he were the injured party. "I thought we were friends."

"That's funny," I told him. "I made the exact same mistake."

Lily Chu

My role at the ceremony was simple: I had to present the bronze plaque to Front Desk Diane. That was it. Just smile and hand it to her. Nate was doing the same thing for Vito Falcone. That was the only reason we were up onstage.

The Superintendent got up first and gave a big shout-out to Kyle Dorfman, who was the "driving force" behind the brand-new Green Meadow High School Hall of Fame, the institution we were about to inaugurate.

"Thank you, Kyle, for your creative vision and extraordinary generosity. We wouldn't be here tonight without you."

Mr. Dorfman pressed his hands together and bowed to the audience. He was on the other side of the podium from me—the all-male side—between Nate and Vito Falcone. Dr. Bramwell's empty chair was over there too.

"And now," he said, "I'd like to hand over the reins to our Assistant Principal, Tracy Flick."

Dr. Flick got up and walked to the podium. She didn't stop to thank the Superintendent or shake his hand; she just brushed right past him, like he wasn't there. She looked good in her little black dress, nothing like her usual wardrobe.

I wish I could tell you what she said, but I was too focused on the reserved seats in the first row, where Clem was sitting between my parents. It was weird to see the three of them like that, almost like they were the family and I was the one who was separate. I wanted to look at Clem, but my eyes kept drifting over to my mother. It was like her face was a magnet, tugging on my guilty conscience.

I'd snuck into Clem's room the night before. I waited until one in the morning, and then I tiptoed across the hall, holding my breath. I shut the door so it didn't even click, and then I slipped into bed next to Clem. Neither of us made a sound. We just snuggled—I mean, we did some stuff, but very quietly—and then I tiptoed out an hour later, and there was my mom, standing in the hall, looking right at me. We stared at each other for a few seconds, and then she went back into her bedroom, and I went into mine.

I thought I'd be in trouble in the morning, but she didn't say a word. We ate breakfast together, the way we always did, and it felt like any other day, except that now she knew. It was right there between us, the secret I'd been hiding for so long.

I gave her a small, apologetic smile from the stage, and she gave me a smaller, not very happy smile in return, and I was okay with that, because I could see that she still loved me, and would love me no matter what.

Tracy Flick

I didn't thank Buzz or acknowledge any of the Board Members or politicians in the audience, not even the Mayor. None of that mattered anymore. I just stood there until I had everyone's attention, and then I recited "Ozymandias," a poem I'd memorized for the occasion.

> *I met a traveller from an antique land*
> *Who said: "Two vast and trunkless legs of stone*
> *Stand in the desert. . . .*

I'd first read it back in high school, and it had made a huge impression on me, though not a positive one. Quite the opposite. I found it depressing, and even a little upsetting, because I valued fame and power—I *believed* in them—and I thought those things would save me.

> *"My name is Ozymandias, king of kings:*
> *Look on my works, ye Mighty and despair!"*

More recently, however, I'd come to find the poem oddly comforting, because I'd learned from bitter experience that there was no justice in the world, and that I would never get what I deserved. My mother had been wrong: fame wasn't a reward for your hard work. It was a lottery, pure dumb luck, and it didn't matter anyway, not in the long run. That was the whole point of the poem. There's no such thing as immortality; all our striving is in vain. In the end, we'll all be forgotten, every single one of us, the winners and the losers alike.

239

. . . *Round the decay*
Of that colossal wreck, boundless and bare
The lone and level sands stretch far away.

I didn't say that in my speech, though. It wasn't appropriate for the occasion. What I said was that the poem was undeniably true, but that it wasn't the whole truth. I said that we live in human time, not geological time, and that we have a duty as humans to honor the people among us who've performed great deeds. I said that was why we were here tonight, to pay tribute to two exceptional graduates of Green Meadow High School, individuals who have inspired us with their talent and their generosity of spirit.

"Diane Blankenship and Vito Falcone," I said. "As long as this building stands and this community exists, you will not be forgotten."

Nate Cleary

Before Vito got his plaque, they turned off the lights and showed a short video celebrating his high school football career. This was the moment I'd been waiting for. The video was my baby—I'd found the footage, I'd done all the editing, and I'd chosen the soundtrack, a bunch of cool songs from the early nineties—Nirvana, Weezer, U2, that kind of thing.

The highlights were amazing, one spectacular play after another: Vito lofting a perfect forty-yard pass to Reggie Morrison, who leaves the defenders in the dust; Vito scrambling for a touchdown, dodging one would-be tackler after another; Vito launching an off-balance Hail Mary that Reggie catches with one outstretched hand to win the State Semifinal in 1993. I added cool graphics and cut in lots of images of the cheerleaders and the band and the scoreboard and the crowd going crazy and the refs signaling for another touchdown. I concluded with a full minute of Green Day's "Good Riddance (Time of Your Life)," played over a slide show of Vito as a little kid, Vito in his Pop Warner uniform, Vito at the prom, Vito in a cap and gown, Vito and Reggie with their arms around each other after the last game of their undefeated senior year, both of them sweaty and joyful, grinning the biggest grins you've ever seen, and then the screen goes black and all it says for like five whole seconds is DIRECTED BY NATE CLEARY, and I can't even tell you how good that felt.

Tracy Flick

I didn't watch the video very closely. I was contemplating my future, thinking that maybe everything would work out for the best, that every setback was really a new opportunity. Maybe now I could go back to law school, pass the bar, live the life that I'd meant to live. It wouldn't be easy, starting a demanding new career in my midforties, competing with all the young hotshots, but nothing had ever been easy for me. I would just have to work harder than everyone else and prove myself to the skeptics, the way I always had, and simply refuse to take no for an answer.

I knew I could do it. I was strong and I was smart and I was a fighter. And I believed in myself.

Tracy Flick would be fine.

When the lights came on, I turned away from the screen and found myself staring straight at Vito Falcone. To my surprise, I saw that he was sobbing—his shoulders were heaving and tears were streaming down his face—and at almost the same moment, I realized that I was sobbing too, though I wasn't sure if I was grieving for his squandered promise or my own.

Jack Weede

I hadn't been feeling well all day. I blamed it on stress—it had been emotionally exhausting, spending the night with Diane, trying to imagine what would happen when Alice got back—but my symptoms worsened during the ceremony. My chest started to ache and I couldn't catch my breath. I should've slipped offstage while the video was playing, but I just sat there, because standing up didn't seem like such a great idea, either.

And then the lights came on, and it was too late. The fat cop—Glenn Keeler, the one who'd pulled me over—was moving down the aisle, heading for the stage, and I could see it in his hand. I tried to warn them, but it felt like there was a heavy leather belt strapped around my chest, and it just kept getting tighter and tighter, and when I opened my mouth . . .

Lily Chu

I didn't know where to look. Dr. Flick was crying, Principal Weede was making this weird gurgling noise, and this other man was standing in the orchestra pit, screaming at Vito Falcone. Front Desk Diane grabbed my hand and pulled really hard just as the Principal pitched forward and the man started shooting.

Tracy Flick

Vito was on the floor. His shirt was wet with blood and his face was wet with tears. I was kneeling beside him, pressing on the wound, trying to keep the blood inside his body, but it wouldn't stay there.

"Tracy," he said, very softly, and I was surprised that he remembered my name.

He mumbled something else, but I couldn't hear him—my ears were ringing and someone kept screaming, *Get out of the way! Get out of the way!*—so I leaned my face a little closer.

"I'm sorry," he whispered. His eyes were cloudy and confused. "Please forgive me."

I was about to tell him that I didn't need to, that he hadn't done anything wrong, not to me, but something must have happened, because I wasn't kneeling anymore, and the words just . . .

EPILOGUE:

One Year Later

- 32 -

Lily Chu

I got invited back for the second Hall of Fame ceremony—they're inducting Principal Weede and Dr. Flick, and completing the presentations from the first year—but I'm going to college in Minneapolis, and it's midterms that week, so I won't be able to make it, which is totally fine with me. I don't ever want to set foot in that auditorium again for as long as I live.

Most of the time I'm okay; I don't even think about what happened that night. It helps being in a new place, surrounded by people who've never even heard of Green Meadow High School. I did tell my roommate; I kind of had to. I was having nightmares at the beginning of first semester, and woke up screaming a few times. I also confided in this girl I was seeing in the fall—it didn't work out between us, and I regret sharing my secret with her—but otherwise I've kept it to myself. It feels wrong to turn it into an anecdote, like, *Hey, did I ever tell you about the time I almost got murdered?*

It's over between me and Clem. Not because we wanted to break up, but just because it's too complicated right now. They're doing a junior year abroad in Australia, and even when they get back to Wesleyan, it's not like we're going to be able to get together for the weekend. We still FaceTime every once in a while, but it's hard with the time difference, and a little awkward, like we're slowly turning into strangers. But whatever happens, they were my first love, and

I'll never forget them. Clem helped me to understand who I am, and made me a braver person, and I'll always be grateful for that.

My mom and I never actually talked about Clem, or my sexuality in general. She just gave me a really stern look before we said good-bye at the end of drop-off.

"No dating," she said. "You focus on your schoolwork."

"And no frat parties," my father added.

We were standing right outside my dorm, with lots of other people around. We did a big family hug right out there on the lawn, all three of us, which was completely out of character. We'd never been big huggers, especially not in public. But we were different after the Hall of Fame. You can't live through something like that and stay the same.

I emailed Front Desk Diane and told her how sorry I was to miss the second ceremony, but she told me not to worry about it.

It's fine, honey. And you already gave me the plaque.

It was true: I was still holding on to it when she pulled me off the stage, out of the line of fire. I didn't see anyone get shot, because we were lying flat on the floor behind the curtain the whole time, and she told me not to look. I just heard the pops and the screams. It was over pretty quickly, but we didn't move for a long time, not until the cops came and told us it was safe. When we got to our feet, I handed her the box I was holding. I think we were both in shock.

"This is for you," I told her.

"Oh," she said. "Thank you so much."

They mounted the plaque right on the front of her desk. It's the first thing you see when you walk into the main office.

Diane J. Blankenship, it says. *Class of 1986. "Front Desk Diane." Beloved friend to all, and longtime GMHS receptionist. Always a smile and a kind word for everyone. Our lives are brighter for knowing you.*

There's a bronze cast of her face above the words. It doesn't really look like Diane, but it's still pretty cool.

Nate Cleary

I got into Davidson, but I took a gap year. I've been doing a lot of hiking, mostly by myself, and working part time at REI. I broke up with Kelly over the summer. I got tired of all the whispering.

I'm thinking about majoring in film. I don't know, though. Maybe I'll do premed, go into emergency medicine.

I just felt so helpless.

Watching people die like that.

Kyle Dorfman

It left a bitter taste in my mouth. I was just trying to do something good for the town. It wasn't my fault that it turned into a tragedy, but people still blamed me for it. They didn't say it out loud, but I could feel it in their eyes.

Marissa was pissed at me too. Among other things, she thought I'd treated Tracy Flick very badly, and then she started dredging up my affair with Veronika, which was ancient history and had nothing to do with Tracy. But for Marissa, it was all part of a larger pattern, which was basically me being an asshole. She said I was always using people and then walking away from the messes I created.

"You never take responsibility," she said. "And you're never the one who gets hurt."

I couldn't take it after a while. I flew to Maui in May—I thought I'd spend a couple of weeks chilling with Vijay—but I still haven't gone back. Why would I? It's beautiful out here, every single day, and there's something deeply healing about living near the ocean. The boys came out for a visit in July, and then again over the Christmas holidays, and they love it too, especially the surfing. They took a few lessons, and that was all they needed. I'm learning too, though it's a little harder at my age. But I try to get out every morning, and I'm making some progress, slow but sure.

Vijay and I have been doing mushrooms and talking about a new project. It's a robot dog based on Barky. A companion for the elderly or the lonely, or just for busy people who don't have time to care for a pet.

A Dog When You Need One.

That's our vision.

Alice Weede

I'm glad they're honoring Jack, but I'm not going back for the ceremony. I'm in Utah right now, and I can't drive the RV all the way back to New Jersey. We already had a family funeral, and a memorial service for Jack's friends and colleagues. And besides, I was never really part of his school life. He kept all that to himself.

It's a little sad being out on the road without him, driving through all this beauty. I tell him about it sometimes.

Oh, Jack, look at those mountains . . .

For a while I thought I'd never forgive him. First for being unfaithful, and then for leaving me—leaving the world—before we could go on the adventure we'd dreamed about. I'll admit it, I was a little bitter. I felt like I'd been cheated out of so much happiness in my life.

But I'm not really mad at him anymore. Sometimes I even miss him. It would be nice to have another driver, a warm body next to me at night, a little help with the crosswords. Somebody to look at the stars with. You wouldn't believe the stars out here.

Oh God, Jack. I never knew there were so many.

Tracy Flick

I was shot twice, once in the shoulder and once in the hip. I'm still in a fair amount of pain. I have to use a cane to get around, and still can't raise my left arm higher than my ear, but I'm working hard on my PT, and I'm getting stronger by the day. And believe me, I'm not complaining. I know how lucky I am. Luckier than Vito Falcone and Jack Weede, that's for sure. They were both dead before they got to the hospital.

It was a long, arduous recovery. Three surgeries, a month in rehab, and a summer of bed rest, giving my traumatized body a chance to heal. I couldn't have gotten through it without Marissa's help. I stayed in her ground-floor guest room the whole time—the kids call it Tracy's Room now—and she brought me food and read aloud to me, and at night we watched old movies, or sat out by the pool and listened to music. Sophia joined us for the month of August—she liked the twins and they liked her—and it was almost like we were a family. I'm back in my own house now, but I still spend a lot of time over there on the weekends. Marissa and I cook together, and we go for short walks—I'm trying to get my stamina back—but mainly we just talk and laugh and keep each other company. Life is so much better with a friend.

I wasn't a hundred percent when September rolled around, but I went back to work anyway. I wouldn't have missed that first day for the world. An honor guard of kids and teachers and custodians and cafeteria workers lined up outside the main entrance, and they all applauded as I limped into the building. The first thing I saw was a big, hand-lettered banner taped to the wall.

WE LOVE YOU, PRINCIPAL FLICK!

That's right: *Principal Flick.*

Everything changed after I got shot. The Board passed a resolution commending me for my heroism and grace under pressure, Larry Holleran withdrew his candidacy, and that was that. It's going pretty well. I've made it very clear that there's a new sheriff in town, and that mediocrity won't be tolerated, not on my watch. It helped that the football team had a great season, thanks to Marcus Turner. We won seven and only lost three, and even made it to the playoffs for the first time in years. Nobody's complaining about Skippy Martino anymore.

Oh, and guess what else? I got elected to the Hall of Fame. They had to change the rules to include people who worked at the school, not just graduates, but that wasn't a problem, because they wanted to make Jack Weede eligible as well. That was sad, Jack dying so suddenly, a massive heart attack just a couple of months before his retirement.

A big part of my job has been helping the kids to process their grief and move towards healing. We hired a full-time counselor, and the kids have come up with some rituals of their own. They've turned Vito's old locker into a kind of shrine. They leave flowers for him sometimes, birthday cards, bags of candy on Halloween, a Christmas stocking with his name on it. In November, a woman named Paige Ellmann came to see it. She said she knew Vito from Florida, and that they'd dated for a little while before his death. I took a picture of her standing next to the plaque, and she took one of me. She hugged me before she left.

"Thank you so much," she said. "That was so brave what you did that night. I'm glad he had someone to comfort him at the end. He was such a lovely man. I miss him every day."

"I wish I could have done more," I said. "I'm sorry for your loss."

It's always a little awkward when people tell me how brave I was, because I can't remember much about what happened that night. The doctors say it's traumatic amnesia, very common among victims of accidents and violent crimes.

A lot of people in the audience took videos, though. You can probably find some of them on the internet, not that I'd recommend it. I clicked on a few, but only because I wanted to fill the holes in my memory. Most of the footage was shaky and out of focus, but there was one video that held still and caught it all.

You can see the shooter moving down the aisle, shouting at Vito and raising his gun, and you can see Jack trying to stand up, his face contorted with pain. And then Vito gets shot—the first bullet knocks him right off his chair—and everyone panics. Diane and Lily flee to the left, Buzz and Kyle and Nate to the right. I don't fault them for that. They did the sensible thing and tried to save themselves. Only Vito and Jack and I remained onstage—Vito on his back, still moving a little, and Jack flat on his face, utterly motionless. I don't know why I didn't try to help him; he was right next to me. I must have known he was dead, though I didn't check for a pulse or anything. I didn't even look at him. I just went straight to Vito.

You can see it on the video.

I get down on my hands and knees, and I crawl over to him, which also means I'm crawling towards the killer, who keeps yelling at me to get out of the way, because he doesn't want to hurt me. But I keep going, and try to help Vito, but there's not much I can do.

At this point, you can see our School Resource Officer, Allison Fitzpatrick, coming down the side aisle. When she gets near the stage, she draws her own weapon and takes a few precious seconds to position herself in a two-handed crouch. The killer takes advantage of that brief hesitation to fire again, and those are the shots that hit me, and a split second later, Allison pulls the trigger and he goes down. It's over.

I must have watched that video twenty or thirty times, but it didn't help as much as I thought it would. I still can't tell you why I did that—why I crawled over to a person I barely knew, got between him and a crazed gunman, and shielded him with my body, as if he were my own child—except to say that that's me, that's who I am, that's how I've tried to live my life. Going where I'm needed, doing what I can to make things better, trying to be of service.

Before you get inducted into the Hall of Fame, they give you an advance look at the inscription on your plaque to make sure you like it. Here's what mine will say: *Dr. Tracy Flick. Educator, Administrator, Friend, and Guide. Fearless Leader with a Big Heart. A True Hero and an Inspiration to Us All.*

After I read those words, I sat at my desk and wept. And then I signed off on the approval form, because I was so touched by the praise, and because it was impossible to ask for more.

Acknowledgments

I'm grateful to so many people for their help with this book—Kathy Belden, Nan Graham, Sylvie Rabineau, Michael Taeckens, Albert Berger, and Ron Yerxa, among others. Special thanks to Maria Massie, my wonderful agent and friend, who knew Tracy Flick from the very beginning, almost thirty years ago now. And to Mary, Luke, Nina, and Jeremy, who were the best pandemic companions anyone could have asked for.

About the Author

Tom Perrotta is the bestselling author of ten works of fiction, including *Election* and *Little Children*, both of which were made into critically acclaimed movies, and *The Leftovers* and *Mrs. Fletcher*, which were both adapted into HBO series. He lives outside Boston.